P9-DEZ-593

SARAH THE DRAGON LADY

MARTHA BENNETT STILES has written a number of books for young readers. She lived for many years in Ann Arbor, Michigan, before moving to her present home in Bourbon County, Kentucky.

Avon Books are available at special quantity discounts for bulk purchases for sales promotions, premiums, fund raising or educational use. Special books, or book excerpts, can also be created to fit specific needs.

For details write or telephone the office of the Director of Special Markets, Avon Books, Dept. FP, 105 Madison Avenue, New York, New York 10016, 212-481-5653.

SARAH THE DRAGON LADY

Martha Bennett Stiles

AN AVON CAMELOT BOOK

To my dazz niece, Diana Mears

AVON BOOKS
A division of
The Hearst Corporation
105 Madison Avenue
New York, New York 10016

Copyright © 1986 by Martha Bennett Stiles
The song "On, On, U of K" appearing on page 44, words by Troy L. Perkins, music by Carl A. Lampert, copyright © 1962 by Paxwin Music, is reprinted by permission of the publisher.
Published by arrangement with Macmillan Publishing Company
Library of Congress Catalog Card Number: 86-8411
ISBN: 0-380-70471-4

All rights reserved, which includes the right to reproduce this book or portions thereof in any form whatsoever except as provided by the U.S. Copyright Law. For information address Macmillan Publishing Company, 866 Third Avenue, New York, New York 10022.

First Avon Camelot Printing: February 1988

CAMELOT TRADEMARK REG. U.S. PAT. OFF. AND IN OTHER COUNTRIES, MARCA REGISTRADA, HECHO EN U.S.A.

Printed in the U.S.A.

OPM 10 9 8 7 6 5 4 3 2 1

1

The Worst Day in My Life

In June this year, I left New York City and came to Meterboro, Kentucky. I didn't want to come, but at least I hoped that fourth grade in Meterboro would be better for me than third grade in New York had been. In third grade, one terrible thing happened to me after another. Each thing was worse than the one before. My last day in third grade wasn't just the worst day I have ever had in school; it was the worst day of my life.

My bad year started the day Jane Jones said I made her spoil our project. "Doesn't sound very bad compared to falling out of a ten-story window," said my father when I complained. He and my mother should both have been on my side; they are supposed to *care* about art.

Jane and I were drawing a picture on the blackboard for a prehistory unit. Jane draws better than I do, so when she said, "I'll do the caveman and the cavewoman and their dog and their baby, and you do the cave and fire and sun and clouds," all I said was, "Where do you want the fire?"

On top of the fire I put the cavemen's lunch, a mastodon

foot. I also put birds in one of my clouds. I put at least one bird in all my pictures. They are sort of a signature with me, like an alligator on a tennis shirt. My mother used to be an artist, and she says plenty of artists do something like that.

After Jane finished her family, she started to draw a thick, black edge all around the cave baby. At the university where our teacher, Miss Sanchez, went to learn how to teach us, somebody told her that pictures show up better if everything in them is outlined. The day my class made Thanksgiving drawings, Miss Sanchez came down the aisles, looking at our work. I heard her telling Magda Wyzack about firm black outlines, and I saw Magda take a crayon and make a thick mark all around her perfectly good Indian. Magda Wyzack has cheeks like pink marshmallows and a nature to match, soft and sweet. She would never argue with a teacher.

I had drawn a blooming pumpkin plant. You were supposed to know that the blossoms would make pumpkins and the pumpkins would make pies, and this was supposed to make you thankful. In one corner I put a little brown bird looking for a pumpkin seed to eat right away. "Very good, Sarah," Miss Sanchez said. "Now you should make your picture more distinct, like this." She didn't even ask; she just took my own crayon and started ruining my picture.

"Hey, don't!" I squawked, and the whole class quit work and looked. "Do you *see* pumpkin vines that way?" I asked her. "Do you *feel* that way about pumpkin vines?" Those are the questions my mother has taught me to ask myself about what I am drawing.

Miss Sanchez and I told each other honestly what we thought about our disagreement, which is another thing my mother has taught me people should do, and in the end Miss Sanchez said, "Very well, Sarah, if you are satisfied with leaving your picture undefined," and went on down the aisle showing everybody else about firm black outlines. I explained all this to my parents when I took the picture home with a *C* on it.

"It's not as if you were painting cathedral walls to last a thousand years," my father said. "Why don't you outline just what you draw for Miss Sanchez? Probably next year you'll have a teacher with different ideas. Some things are more important than crayon drawings."

My mother looked grim. I couldn't tell if she was displeased with me for getting a *C*, or with Miss Sanchez for being such a moron, or with my father for saying that crayon drawings, which my mother makes a lot of, are not important. I wish I'd asked her before the day Jane started outlining her cave baby.

"Miss Sanchez says you're supposed to finish pictures this way," Jane told me.

"On a blackboard," I pointed out, "everything is already outlined in black." Jane stood there rolling the black chalk between her thumb and fingers. "You can mess up your own stuff if you want to," I told her, "but keep that dumb black chalk away from mine."

Whenever our class finished a unit, we would have project evaluation. This meant that Miss Sanchez would start with the person at the front left-hand desk (*always*) and work back, then up the next aisle and down the next, asking each person what the project's good points were and how it needed to be improved. (Magda Wyzack always said something complimentary, no matter what a total mess the project was.)

When the time came to evaluate Jane's and my cavemen blackboard, Miss Sanchez started where she *never* starts, with the boy in the last seat in the right-hand row. Our picture was on the front left-hand corner blackboard, so that seat was the farthest from it in the room. To begin with, that boy was not interested in anything except baseball. He always answered teachers' questions, "I did know, but I forgot," or, "I know, but I can't put it in words." He was half-asleep, probably dreaming about a home run, when Miss Sanchez asked, "Harry, what do you think about the picture?"

"Which pitcher?" he said.

Miss Sanchez didn't snap "Wake up!" at him the way she usually did. "Can't you see it very well, Harry?" she asked.

For a few seconds Harry didn't say anything. Maybe he hoped someone would whisper to him what Miss Sanchez was talking about. Instead somebody giggled, and Harry said, "No, ma'am."

"Of course you can't see it," Miss Sanchez said, "and the reason is that Sarah and Jane did not choose to remember what I showed you all about outlining your figures."

Jane's face got red. "I started to do it," she said, "but Sarah made me stop!"

"If Sarah told you to stop getting out from in front of a swift truck," Miss Sanchez asked, "would you sit down?" The class laughed.

I thought Jane was going to cry. "Well, I wanted to do what you said," she whined, "but Sarah yelled at me. She got real mad, and she said my drawing was *dumb!*"

"Sarah likes her own way," Miss Sanchez said, as if that were something special about me. That's what "your own way" *means*—how you like things. I don't always expect my own way, but I'd have to be dead not to want it. "Sarah is very pleased with her ideas about art, class," Miss Sanchez went on. "Let's see how pleased we are." She called on the girl who sat right in front of Harry, Nancy Quisenberry, who isn't even as smart as he is. At least Harry can hit a ball.

"Why is the sun shining when it's raining?" Nancy asked.

"It's not raining," I said.

4

"What are those black squiggles in the big cloud?"

I waited for somebody else to tell her, but everybody just looked at me. "Those are buzzards, gathering over where the cavemen made their kill," I said. Everybody laughed, and they were not laughing at Nancy.

Up that aisle and down the next, everybody thought Jane's and my picture was terrible, and everybody thought it was my fault, for being stubborn and stuck-up. My eyes and nose began to sting, and I had to put my elbows on my desk and my fists under my chin to prop it up high so nothing would slide down. When Fred Ranck said, "Why is the biggest log on top of the fire instead of on the bottom?" I didn't try to explain about my mastodon foot. I just began to repeat silently to myself, Magda will say something good. Magda will say something good.

"I think the buzzards are a true-to-life idea," Magda said. That is why, when my mother and I came down here to Kentucky, Magda was the first one at home I wrote.

When I was little I had a baby-sitter who, every time I scratched or bumped myself, used to comfort me by saying, "It will be well before you are married." This was no help at all and made no more sense than if she had sung "Jingle Bells." I was glad when she moved to New Jersey and couldn't sit me anymore. Now that I am older, I understand that what she meant was, "Some hurts don't hurt forever." (Why couldn't she have said that?) A bruise or a scratch goes away, to make room for the next one, and you forget about it once you aren't purple and green or scabby anymore. Some things, though, are so terrible that they never go away. Even if you never get married or get married a thousand times, you will never forget them. That's what my last day in third grade was like.

It started out fine. Miss Sanchez was in a good mood because she was never going to have to teach any of us again, and the class was in a good mood because nobody had failed, not even Harry. After Miss Sanchez handed out our final reports, there was nothing we had to do until the bell rang to let us go home. "Well, class," Miss Sanchez asked, "what would you like to do? That is quiet," she added.

"We could have a spelling match," I suggested. I am really good at spelling.

Somebody groaned. Most of the kids made faces. "Has someone read a book she'd like to tell us about?" Miss Sanchez asked.

A lot more kids groaned. "Why don't we vote," Fred Ranck suggested, "on who should give us a book report?"

Magda had to come to the front of the room because she was president, and the president has to take nominations and count votes.

Most of my classmates in third grade didn't give very good book reports. Jane was worst; she told what happened in every single paragraph. One night after Jane gave a report, I dreamed I was trapped in an elevator that, instead of playing music, was playing "and then, and then, and then, and then," and I was never going to die. At least the other kids made their reports short.

The first time Miss Sanchez made us write book reports, she wrote four questions on the blackboard that she said we could ask ourselves when we judged a book. Everybody copied the list.

DOES THE AUTHOR USE LOCAL COLOR WELL?
DOES THE AUTHOR KNOW THE CHARACTERS?
IS THE STORY BELIEVABLE, THAT IS, IS IT
    TRUE-TO-LIFE?
DOES THE STORY TEACH YOU SOMETHING?

6

The first time she called on us to read our reports aloud, Harry went first. "My book is *Jake,* by Alfred Slote. Alfred Slote uses local color well in his book. He really knows his characters. I learned something from this book."

Magda went next. "My book is *Tom Savage in the New World,* by Peggy Wells," she said. "This author uses local color very well and she really knows her characters. I think her story is very true-to-life. I learned a lot from this book."

There were two more exactly like Harry's and Magda's, *and then* Jane gave hers until the bell rang for recess.

I am always reading at least two books. I keep one under my pillow and another under the towels in the bathroom closet, and I don't mind telling anybody what they are about. When I finally had my turn, I could tell that the class liked my report, but I didn't know how much until the last day of school when Magda asked for nominations and Fred said, "I nominate Sarah," and Nancy said, "I second the nomination," and Harry said, "I move the nominations be closed," and the ayes had me.

The trouble was, I needed to go to the bathroom. I knew if I asked to go they'd never wait for me, and I was so thrilled that Fred Ranck had nominated me and the whole class had voted for me that I was not going to leave and have them elect somebody else. I just knew I would get back from the girls' room and Jane would be standing where I should have been, and it wouldn't make any difference whether the class still wanted me, because she would never quit in time for somebody else to go next; she would never quit till school ended for the whole year, and next year I would be in a different class. I decided to walk up to the front very fast, because sometimes walking fast will help.

My idea worked, for maybe a minute. Then the feeling came back. I was already giving my report and everybody in the room was looking at me, even Harry. I sucked in the way I do to put on tight jeans, which made it difficult to talk, but which helped some. I crossed one leg in front of the other and pushed them together as hard as I could. Maybe I sort of rocked back and forth a little. "I've never seen you so fidgety, Sarah," Miss Sanchez said. Then I felt it happen.

I tried to go on talking as though nothing hot was trickling down my leg. I couldn't do a thing about it, and now I couldn't go back to my desk, either. I began to slow my book report down. I began to tell more and more of what happened. "And then," I said, "and then . . ." The kids looked at me as if I had lost my wits. Even Miss Sanchez began to fiddle with her pencil. I went on telling. "And then," I said. I could imagine what was going to happen when I finished and started back toward my seat. *Miss Sanchez, look at Sarah's jeans!* "And then," I said. The kids began shifting in their seats. Fred Ranck was drawing airplanes. Harry was rolling a baseball on his desktop and Miss Sanchez didn't say anything to him about it. "And then," I said. And then the bell rang.

All the kids jumped up, whooping. Miss Sanchez began yelling at them to go quietly. I stood where I was, waiting for everybody to be gone. I knew I didn't have any hope that my jeans would be dry before I had to leave, but at least I could wait till everyone I knew was far away. Miss Sanchez followed the other kids out in the hall to be sure they didn't run inside the building, but then she came back.

"Is something the matter, Sarah?" she asked.

"I just wanted to stand here a minute."

She looked worried, and I knew it wasn't just about me. Teachers like to go home, too. "You look as if you don't feel well."

"I'm just sad," I said, my second fib. "I'm just sad that school is over till September."

Her face relaxed so much, she was almost pretty. She looked friendlier than she had looked when looking at *me* since November (when she spoiled my pumpkin picture). She put her arm around me. I had to make myself stiff or I would have been turned around by this hug, and Miss Sanchez stopped smiling and took her arm away and said, "Well, Sarah, I'm sure you will find ways to have a nice summer." I had never felt so terrible in my life. I didn't have any idea that things were going to get even worse, and soon.

At home I told my mother, "I hate that school. I don't ever want to go back to that school, never, ever." My mother didn't ask one question. She said, "Well, Sarah. . . ." I didn't know she had already made plane reservations to Kentucky: just two—one for her and one for me. She didn't make any for my father. When I found that out, it was an even worse day than the worst day in my life.

2

Worst Gets Worse

My mother used to be an artist. Now she is an illustrator. (The difference, she says, is that illustrators get paid.)

My father is a fashion designer. He has his own showroom. His collections always make an important statement. He uses only authentic fabrics. He has to live in New York City, he says, and nowhere else. Certainly not, for instance, in Kentucky. "I would starve in Kentucky," my father says. Sometimes I am afraid that is exactly what my mother and I will end up doing.

The night after what I thought was the worst day of my life, I went to bed with a good book that I hoped would make me forget all about what had happened to me at school the day before. After a while I heard my parents talking in their room next door, and before I had read six pages, something about my father's tone of voice made me turn off my flashlight and throw the sheet off my head. What they were discussing was, a book publisher had asked my mother to draw the pictures for a story about horses in Kentucky.

"Are there no horses in New York?" my father asked. "Does the New York Public Library take no horse magazines? Surely if Degas painted horses from photographs, you can."

Degas is my mother's favorite painter. She has shown me some of his pictures in New York, but there are a lot more in Paris, France, where he lived, she says, and someday she will get to see them. She says he didn't always paint from photographs; he spent hours at the racetrack. "I can't draw Kentucky in New York," she told my father.

She never thought she had to leave New York before, when she illustrated a book. "What about *me*?" my father asked her.

"I didn't say 'What about me?' when you took your spring line to Tokyo," she said. "I didn't say, 'Photographs are just as good. Just send the Japanese some photographs of your clothes.'"

"Oh, that's it," said my father. "You know it was totally impractical to take you to Tokyo."

"And it's not practical to take you to Kentucky," said my mother, "but Sarah and I are going."

I sat up! They didn't know I heard everything they said right through my bedroom wall even with a pillow over my head, and that night I didn't put a pillow over my head.

"Do you mean to tell me you have already promised this publisher and signed his contract and taken his advance money without a word to me?" my father demanded.

"You didn't check out my wishes before you made your plans for Tokyo," said my mother. "You just said, 'We're going,' and 'we' didn't mean me, it meant umpteen of those females who work for you."

"Well," said my father. "I assume you will be back in your home in time for Sarah's school."

"Sarah will go to school in Kentucky," my mother told him, "just the way your nephew goes to school in Florida every winter." It's a good thing I wasn't standing up. I might have fainted.

My father's brother takes my aunt and cousin to Florida for three months every winter, and my cousin goes to a special school for migrants like him. I don't believe there even are any schools like that in Kentucky.

Of course, I didn't believe my father would put my mother and me on an airplane bound for Blue Grass Field without him, either, but he did.

There was nobody to meet us. My mother didn't know anybody in Kentucky any more than I did. We took a limousine to the bus station in Lexington and a Greyhound bus to Meterboro and a taxi to Simon Kenton Street, where we are borrowing a house from somebody who was my mother's friend in art school before I was born. This friend lives in Chicago; she inherited the house on Simon Kenton Street from her great-aunt. She is glad we are in the house, because when it is empty she is always afraid that the roof will start leaking and nobody will put a pan under it, or something.

Mrs. Hume was the first person I met in Kentucky; she is in charge of the Meterboro Public Library. She says she is the only person who goes there more often than I do. Whether my mother is being an artist or an illustrator, when she is doing a picture with a child in it, I pose for her. Sometimes I have to stand on one foot while holding something ridiculous out in front of me, and once I even had to stand on my head, but whatever she's having me do, I have to do it forever at a time, and not move. If I itch or sneeze or need to go to the bathroom, my mother reminds me that I like to eat, too. When I see that my mother is going to be putting a child into what she is working on, I go to the library and don't come home till time for the next meal—except on days when something has reminded her that I have a room and she has inspected

12

it and I am not allowed to leave this house until . . .

Mrs. Hume calls me Sarah, like my mother. My father calls me Heron-Hips. My father's models get paid, and they get to walk around, too. I can never be a fashion model because my nose is too squatty, but it is true I am no fatter than a leaf.

The leaves were almost green-black when my mother and I first got here. Now they've mostly fallen. The vine that winds through the tree that I see from my window has turned the color of the wine my father and mother used to drink with hamburgers. The tree is a linden. There are trash trees and worthwhile trees, Mrs. Hume says. She says the linden is a worthwhile tree.

This linden shades the corner where Simon Kenton Street meets up with Henry Clay Street, the corner our mailman comes around. Mrs. Hume says no, Henry Clay was not Simon Kenton's friend, because they were born in different centuries, but she says they both had plenty of other friends.

The second day I went to the library, I saw a girl in blue denim shorts and a shirt the color of that vine I mentioned, listening to records through earphones. She looked about my age. She had black hair, braided—the kind of braid my father is putting on his total fall line, but thicker—and her eyebrows were like two charcoal drawing sticks laid end to end. I couldn't see what color her eyes were because she was listening with them closed. Her initials were embroidered on her shirtfront like Reddiwhip on raspberry sherbet: A.F.

Right away I got a book and took it out on the grass in front of the library to read. My plan was to ask that girl what A.F. stood for. Then she could ask me my name if she wanted to, and I could ask her where she lived, and maybe it would be in my direction and we could walk home together.

I waited till I had patterns on the undersides of my legs, but when A.F. finally did come out she never even saw me.

There was a vermilion bicycle leaning against the library wall; she got on it and pedaled away.

Mrs. Hume told me the girl's name was Annette Frazier and that I didn't have to be so conscientious about the NO TALKING IN THE LIBRARY sign.

It pleased me when Mrs. Hume called me conscientious; conscientious is something my mother says I should be more. I should be more conscientious about my room because it is my self-space, and I should be important to myself. "You can't stay in touch with your feelings when you're surrounded by disharmony," she says. We came to Kentucky so my mother could get in touch with her feelings, about my father.

I should be more conscientious about being around when she needs me to pose because I like to eat, too.

The first time I told my mother my tooth hurt, she said I should be more conscientious about brushing. "I have to give up the morning and take you to the dentist," she said, "and the light isn't right anymore by afternoon."

The next time I had to go, though, she didn't complain.

Dr. Bedford, my dentist, is the second person I met in Meterboro. I hoped he would have some children my age, but he isn't married.

Dr. Bedford has lived in Meterboro all his life. He told my mother that it is a known fact that ninety percent of the people in Meterboro have lived here all their lives.

Dr. Bedford gave me an appointment to come back after my X rays were developed. It was in the morning like my first appointment, but my mother didn't say anything to him about early light.

Dr. Bedford knows a lot of known facts, which he tells my mother. Now that he has fixed my tooth, he comes to our house to tell her. He wears a T-shirt that says THINK SNOW over a pair of crossed skis.

14

"How does Dr. Bedford think we think he could tell us an *unknown* fact?" I asked my mother. That was one of the mornings when she went upstairs and inspected my room (from the doorway, she said, which was as far as she could get, she said) and I wasn't allowed to *leave this house until*.

That was the day the hummingbird built her nest. (The hummingbird is a worthwhile bird, Mrs. Hume says. It eats spiders.) She built it in the mimosa tree that grows right under my window. The mimosa has leaves like dark green lace fans and flowers like pink powder puffs, and I can see the nest in it because I watched the hummingbird build it and I know where to look, but I am careful not to look now because it is empty now.

In New York I live in an apartment building that doesn't have a yard, let alone a tree. "See," says my mother, "that's something you can have here we didn't have before."

If my father looked out my window, he would go to his drafting table and next thing you know he would bring home a new bolt of cotton printed green and pink and *like* a mimosa tree, but surprising, and he would give me and my friends scraps to tie around our necks. I have several friends in New York.

I look out my window while I'm dressing. I have to change clothes a lot, because my mother is always needing me to put on this or that when I pose for her. So I'm bored with always getting dressed in something, and *that* is why I look out the window so much. I don't have any, you know, particular reason. I mean, I don't have to look out the window.

Sometimes I happen to be looking when the mailman comes around the corner, and then, of course, I'm bound to notice whether he turns up our walk. I put both my hands over my mouth, and if I don't breathe until he is beside our gate, he will turn in. It hasn't worked every time. Maybe my nose leaks.

When my mother first told me that she and I were coming to Meterboro, she said it wouldn't be so bad to leave my friends; she said they would write to me if I wrote to them. I wrote to all of them the first week I got here.

My father writes me sometimes, and he writes my mother a lot. Most of his letters to me are the same. "Be a good girl and don't fill up your interior space with junk," he always says.

You probably think he means pizza, but he means books whose illustrations he doesn't like and facts that are not beautiful, whether they are known or not.

And he always says I should be true to myself and happy with myself. I'd rather be happy with my friends. I never did get a letter from any of them.

I don't know if my father always says the same things to my mother. I've only seen one of his letters to her, that is, one page of one of his letters to her. They are always many pages long, and I guess my mother didn't notice when this one page fell off the table in our eating space while we were having lunch.

After we ate, my mother had to get right back to her easel because she had a deadline, and she said if I would clear the table for her, I could go to the library afterward.

"Loneliness is like an invisible dragon," my father wrote my mother. "You don't see it, but it devours you." Devours means to eat you up—guts, too. Guts especially. I put the page on my mother's napkin, and I walked very quickly to the library.

3

Invisible Dragons

I was reading when Annette Frazier walked into the library. Right away I took my book up and asked Mrs. Hume a question about it so I'd be there when Annette came with the books she chose. Mrs. Hume never gives short answers. I already knew how Simon Kenton spent three foodless days totally stark naked in the snowy forests of Kentucky, and how later he bought the entire state of Indiana from Tecumseh, who also offered to sell him Ohio, but not till Simon Kenton had found out that Tecumseh didn't own Indiana or Ohio, either one, and I learned all that just from asking Mrs. Hume whether Simon Kenton and Henry Clay were friends.

When Annette Frazier did come up with her books, I was really happy for a minute, because she had seven big ones and I thought after Mrs. Hume introduced us I could help Annette carry them home. Her house isn't so many blocks beyond my corner; Mrs. Hume had already told me that.

This time Annette's eyes were open, of course; they are green and clear, like lime jelly. She didn't smile when I offered to help her carry her books. She said her father and her little sister were waiting for her in her father's car. Six of the books were for them, she said, and she couldn't keep them waiting. I didn't even get a chance to ask her what the seventh book was.

Then the library closed for the day and I had to go home and my mother wanted me to put on jeans and lean on a pitchfork for half an hour.

Meterboro Elementary is on Henry Clay Street, like Annette Frazier's house, only in the other direction from here. By the first day of school, I knew that Annette would be in fourth grade, too. I also knew that she would have to walk to school like me, because the vermilion bike belongs to her brother; she only got to ride it while he was away at camp. I found out all that the day of the library contest.

The morning school started, I looked out the window while I dressed, the way I always do. I felt all excited when I saw someone in an off-white turtleneck crossing Simon Kenton Street at the corner of Henry Clay, but only for an instant, because the person was almost as tall as my mother.

The hummingbird's eggs were off-white. The nest was like a fairy-tale cradle, no bigger than a walnut shell, and she fastened it to the branch with spiderwebbing. Then she laid these two eggs and sat on them all by herself for two weeks, and then after the little hummingbirds hatched she fed them all by herself. The father hummingbird never came at all. I saw him once, though, before the mother bird laid her eggs. He was so beautiful—his feathers were as shiny as pure lamé, all red and white and green, and *surprising*. My mother said the mother hummingbird didn't need him around, but he was so beautiful.

The little birds never minded when their mother flew off

to find flowers or spiders, because they had each other. I hope my mother's next picture book is about birds.

When I was little, I was afraid people would recognize me in my mother's pictures, but I've learned that the children she paints or draws while I'm in front of her never look like me. When she's an illustrator they're prettier than me, and when she's an artist they're uglier than anybody.

Dr. Bedford says it's a known fact that a person can't have an attractive face without good, well-fitting teeth. I started to tell him about a book about a beautiful princess that my mother illustrated with silhouettes. The princess's teeth don't show at all, of course. He put a tube in my mouth that sucks your spit as if your mouth were a big red flower and the tube were a hummingbird beak. With that tube in my mouth I couldn't talk any more than a flower can, and Dr. Bedford went on telling my mother known facts.

Annette Frazier has good, well-fitting teeth. Her teeth are worthwhile.

The second person who turned our corner while I was dressing for my first day of school in Meterboro had a dog, which Annette Frazier does not have, and anyway this person was too old to be on her way to school, unless she was a teacher, and a teacher would not take a dog to school.

This woman's dog was wearing a pink plastic collar with rhinestones, the kind my father would call totally vulgar. When the dog made them stop beside the linden tree, the woman pretended to see a bird. Maybe the dog's pee will kill the vine. My mother says the vine is killing the tree—"suffocating it, like the wrong relationship." I asked her why she doesn't chop the vine off at the roots, then. "I'm trying," she said, but I haven't seen her try; we don't even have a hatchet. All she does is paint.

If I had a dog he would wear authentic leather only.

I have never had any pet, because my mother works at home and a dog or a cat would interrupt her and distract her worse than my father and I do, not to mention certainly messing up her things. I don't have to have a pet.

I didn't even have to have one when the library had a pet contest.

I was the first one who saw Mrs. Hume's sign about the contest, because I was there when she tacked it up. Right away I planned to come. I didn't know then whether Annette Frazier had a pet, but I knew lots of children would show up. When the day came, I was waiting when Mrs. Hume got to the library. "We're going to have the contest here on the grass, Sarah," she told me. I sat under a bush, and before long the yard was full. Annette was on the other side of the yard from me. "Everyone must bring his pet up front and tell us about it," Mrs. Hume said. "One at a time, please. Then we will vote on which is best."

The first dog looked like a weimaraner. My cousin in New York has a weimaraner; it always licked my face. The boy who brought this dog said it was a vizsla. "A vizsla costs more than ten Atari cartridges," he bragged. Nobody clapped for him very much.

Then a girl in orange sandals and an orange sundress with lace on the straps got up with a big dog the color of our yard after my mother and I forgot to sprinkle it. "My dog is an Airedale," she said. "An Airedale can sniff out a bomb that a murderer might hide on an airplane where the police wouldn't have been able to find it without him." I could tell by the way everybody clapped that this girl had a lot of friends in Meterboro.

Annette Frazier's hands were empty, like mine. "My dog is a saluki," she said. "Salukis are the fastest dogs in the world.

My saluki runs faster than light; that's why you can't see her."
Mrs. Hume clapped very loudly. I clapped till my hands stung.
I didn't know whether Annette could see me clapping or not.

Then Mrs. Hume called on me.

"My pet is an invisible dragon," I said. One girl giggled,
but most of the children just stared at me. I couldn't look at
Annette Frazier. "No facts are known about dragons," I said,
"which can be the best thing about them or the worst." I was
going to sit down, but nobody was clapping; so I said something more that I had just thought of. "My dragon's back is
so long and broad, two people could ride to school on his
back—and he would wait all day and ride us home again."

The girl in the orange sundress won the prize, which was
a book about horses. Everybody else got an apple out of a
basket in front of the library door.

Annette came up to me before I even bit into mine. "Would
you like a ride home?" she asked. "There's room in our car
for you, but your dragon will have to run alongside."

"If I can hold his leash through the window," I said. "I
never know who will get devoured if I don't hang on tight."
When Annette laughs, her eyes shine like sunlight flashing
off a hummingbird's back.

Mrs. Frazier was wearing braids like Annette's, only pinned
up, and Army coveralls. "This is Sarah," Annette told her.
"She keeps a dragon tied to the tree in her front yard, when
she isn't riding him to the library."

"That's nice," said Mrs. Frazier. "Fasten your seatbelts,
please, girls."

I live so close to the library that by the time we got our
belts buckled we were at my house, and I couldn't invite
Annette and her mother inside because I knew my mother
was working.

After that, whenever I went to the library and heard the

door open, I promised myself that if I didn't breathe before I saw the person who had opened it, it would be Annette, and she would be looking for me; but it never was.

When I wrote my father that the nest in my mimosa is empty, he wrote back that hummingbirds go to Mexico every single winter. I wonder if they find their friends when they get there, or if they spend the whole winter alone?

Those big orange butterflies go to Mexico, too, my father says, and just sleep till spring. He didn't mention dragons, whether they ever leave.

Annette knows where I live, and she has to come right past my corner on her way to school. My first school morning my mother started yelling up the stairs that I would be late, but I did not answer; I was holding my breath. Someone was coming around the corner of Henry Clay Street.

It was Annette, and she was walking on my side of the street.

She turned into our yard, where my dragon had gone sound asleep in the red and white and green and always surprising sunlight.

4
Feeling GOOD

Last year my father got my birthday present at Scribner's and I got his at Gristedes'. My father loves cream puffs and macaroons and chocolate éclairs, and especially chocolate éclairs with a raspberry sauce that has a French name my father knows how to pronounce. This sauce is hard for even the best chefs to make, but my father said I did a very good job of making it for him, American style, on his birthday last year. I stirred a quarter of a cup of frozen orange juice into half a jar of raspberry jam and heated them till they boiled. Then I poured one soup-ladleful over two chocolate éclairs, which I had bought myself with my allowance, and served them to my father on his favorite plate. He said he liked it even better than the *gateau* his staff had given him at lunch.

In New York there are lots of bookstores, not just Scribner's, and lots of delicatessens besides Gristedes'. In Meterboro there is no bookstore and no delicatessen and, until my mother finishes these pictures she came down here to draw, no allowance.

When my mother told my father that I would go to fourth grade in Kentucky, he was totally not pleased. "Sarah can't be just jerked in and out of school like an apple picker," he said. "Or were you planning to spend all year?"

If I were an apple picker, I could earn some money for birthday presents.

"Your brother takes his child to Florida for three months every single winter," my mother said, "and I've never heard you call your nephew an apple picker." She didn't answer the part about was she planning to spend all year.

Totally nothing for me in Kentucky is like Florida for my cousin. In his Florida school, all the kids are strangers. In Meterboro, everybody at my school was born in Meterboro except me. Also, my cousin always knows exactly when he is going back to New York because my uncle always goes back to his office after exactly three months. All my mother tells me is, "We'll see," and I have already been in Kentucky more than three months. In the third place, both my cousin's parents go to Florida. They keep right on giving him his allowance, too.

When my mother finishes this book, the publisher will pay her a lot of money. (My father says it is not a lot, but my mother and I think it is.) He already paid her some before she even started to work, so she could pay for plane tickets to Kentucky, and things like food and paper and fixative while she is working on his book. (Fixative is a spray you spray on charcoal drawings so they won't smear. My mother uses a lot of it.) He didn't give her enough for her to rent a place for us to live in down here, but that was okay because my mother's friend doesn't charge us any rent. Before we came she was worried sick about nobody being here to keep raccoons and burglars out. We have to pay for a lot of things, though, like water and electricity, and our apartment in New York doesn't cost any less just because we aren't in it. I haven't had any allowance since June.

One day I realized it was almost time for my father's birthday, and here I was in Kentucky with no money. I told Annette about it as we walked home from school. "You could make him a card," Annette said.

"I can't draw," I answered, and I can't. This summer I promised to draw Mrs. Hume a picture of the hummingbird in our mimosa tree, but when I tried, my picture looked like a blimp that got its nose stuck in a plumber's plunger and crash-landed on a branch. "That's very good for your age," my mother said. *For your age* means totally rotten.

I remembered about her silhouette princess, and I tried a silhouette for Mrs. Hume, but it was terrible. Color is the whole point of a hummingbird. You couldn't even tell what was sitting in the tree. I proved this by taking my picture to my mother and telling her it was a cat. "That's very good for your age, Sarah," she said.

I took Mrs. Hume a piece of my mother's black art paper. "This is my hummingbird at midnight," I said.

Mrs. Hume laughed. "You're a clever duck, Sarah," she said.

I told Annette all this while we walked home, except I left out about the clever duck. "I just can't draw," I said again.

A teacher would have answered, *You can draw if you try,* but Annette said, "You can paste. You can cut and paste and print. Simms"—Simms is her brother, the one whose bike she rides when he is at camp—"Simms got a birthday card from a girl in his class that said HI! FEEL BELOW! and underneath it said G O O D in fuzzy orange stuff, and inside the card it said, 'Just had to be sure you felt good on your birthday!' "

"Well," I said, "I have some black velvet. It's just a scrap I folded into the bottom of my jewelry box, to make my jewelry look authentic." *Think about the total picture,* my father always says. To make a new line of dresses look worth what he is going to charge for them, he makes the background for his show look very expensive. He drapes velvet over the runway and puts orchids around in pots, things like that. He is right; the scrap of velveteen he gave me makes my necklaces look like an advertisement.

Annette couldn't stop at my house because she had promised to read to Lulu, her little sister, while her mother canned applesauce. Anyway, I had to pose. That night, though, I cut a piece off the back of my velveteen scrap and put it in my spelling book so I wouldn't forget it, and next morning Annette and I worked on my father's birthday card at recess. Instead of just HI! I printed HI DAD! Annette helped me cut out the G, D, and two Os and paste them on. I print better than Annette, but she cuts better. "My hands are strong," she says, "probably from riding."

The book Annette was borrowing that second time I ever saw her turned out to be *Horse and Rider: from Basics to Show Competition*. Annette has a riding lesson every Saturday.

We didn't get the letters pasted perfectly in line, but Annette said that was a plus. "Perfect is plastic," she said.

Annette's mother is a potter, so the Fraziers don't have any plastic dishes in their house. "Imperfections," says Mrs. Frazier, "make a handmade piece *look* handmade."

"I believe my father will like his card," I told Annette. I really did believe so, and also, I didn't want her to think I didn't appreciate her idea when I added, "But I've got to do better for Christmas."

"Will we," I had asked my mother already by the Fourth of July, "be home again by Christmas?"

"We'll see," she had said.

Once when I was little, I asked my mother if I could go somewhere, and she answered, "We'll see." I was standing there on one foot, wondering where to put the other one down, so finally I said, "Does 'We'll see' mean yes or no?" and my mother made me go to my room for being lippy. Usually, I've learned, *We'll see* means *No*, so now I told Annette, "I've got to earn some money between now and December so I can send my father a Christmas present."

"What a good idea," she said. "I need some, too. I'm getting too old to be always giving my parents something I make out of my mother's clay. They're never surprised. I bet Simms would let us help with his paper route. He's always complaining about how much work it is. What will you give your parents?"

"Before my grandmother died she used to send my father a fruitcake every Christmas, and I think he misses them. My mother doesn't have time to bake. I could send him a fruitcake."

"That's a dazz idea." Annette says dazz when she extra likes something; it's short for dazzling. "What will you give your mother?" I didn't want to tell her I wasn't worried about my mother. It was my mother's fault I didn't have any money for presents. If I just made her a card like the one I made for my father for his birthday, that would serve her right. Fortunately the bell rang to end recess and we had to hurry and clean up our paper and velvet scraps and I never answered Annette.

5

Windchill Factor

The next morning was Saturday, and Dr. Bedford came to give my mother a ride to a horse swimming pool so she could draw horses swimming. He was wearing a T-shirt that said WOOD BURNERS ARE WARM PEOPLE. He told my mother that it's a known fact that the snow is just as good at Ski Butler, Kentucky, as at any lodge in New York. "How good is the fireplace?" my mother joked. I was glad I had permission to spend the day at Annette's and could leave.

I didn't tell my mother that I mainly wanted to find out what Simms Frazier thought about Annette and me helping him with his paper route, because she would have asked me what I needed money for.

I think Simms is a funny name for a boy. Where Annette's brother got it is, it was Mrs. Frazier's last name before she married Mr. Frazier. My mother didn't change her name when she married my father. "The people I worked for knew me by my own name," she says, "so it only made sense for me to keep it." I think wives do that more in New York than in Kentucky. In Meterboro I've met a lot of kids whose mothers gave up their last names when they got married, and just called one of their children by it instead. So people still know who they were, just like New York mothers.

Simms didn't like Annette's idea. "You can't go out on the street every morning when it's still dark the way I have to do," he said, "and you don't have bikes."

"Ohh, Simms," Annette wailed. "*How* can Sarah and I make some money? We *have* to."

"You can think of something," Simms said, so I knew he couldn't.

That's when I suggested that Mrs. Hume probably had a shelfful of books on the subject, and Annette and I trudged all the way back down Henry Clay Street to the library. We both watched the gutter all the way for cans or bottles. Annette knows where glass and aluminum can be sold for recycling.

Mrs. Hume gave us *Forty Ways to Buy a Sled,* which was a whole book of ways you could earn money to buy your own sled if your parents wouldn't give you one. "PLAN A CIRCUS!" it suggested. "Charge admission!" All its suggestions ended like that, with exclamation marks. Get all the children in your neighborhood, it went on, to be clowns and fat ladies and elephants. "Design your own clever costumes!"

"I could be a fat lady," I told Annette. "You could wrap a sheet round and round my stomach and then I could put my mother's wrapper on over that." In real life, I am just a bird leg with a human head on top.

"Nobody would come except parents," said Annette. Usually she is hard to discourage, but she had been counting on Simms.

"Then use lots of children," I said, "so lots of parents will come."

"The more children have parts, the more we have to share the money with."

I hadn't thought about giving the other children any of the money. I turned the page to the next suggestion. "SHOVEL SNOW!"

"You've got two snow shovels hanging in your garage," I reminded Annette.

"There won't be any snow in Meterboro before Thanksgiving, and that's too late," she said. "All the Christmas things cost more after Thanksgiving."

I turned the page. "HAVE A COOKIE BAKE! Sell your cookies to your neighbors!" I'm pretty good at making cookies. Last Christmas my father and I made at least three dozen star cookies to hang on our tree.

"Baking is okay," Annette said, "but selling is something else. I've helped my mother sell her pottery at crafts fairs." She raised her chin and prissed her lips, so I knew she was going to be a grown-up. "What kind of clay was this, dear?" she asked in a silly, high voice. I glanced at Mrs. Hume, but Mrs. Hume had forgotten we were in the library. "Will it give me lead poisoning if I cook in it?" Annette was holding *Forty Ways to Buy a Sled* at arm's length and leaning back away from it as if it were a pot full of arsenic crickets that might jump right out into her mouth. I tried not to giggle. "Welll, I don't know," Annette said in that voice. "I really wanted pink. Haven't you got a pink one just like it?" Annette let her own face and voice come back. "Then she says maybe she'll come back later, and it's good-bye, Charlie."

I thought about how tired my mother used to be when she had spent the day going from publisher to publisher with her drawings, looking for an editor who would like them well enough to give her a book to illustrate. I remembered how upset my father was one time when a new magazine had a

30

picture of one of his clients in it, and this woman had been buying all her evening gowns from my father since before I was born, but there she was in a gown made by Frederico. At first I didn't know what was wrong, because my father started out talking about her hair. "Just *hanging*, like *laundry*," he said. "Well, if she wants her face to look dragged down, so be it. It's nothing to me. When you are her age, Sarah, you must wear your hair up, up, high on your head, so people will look at your eyes. You have beautiful eyes. *Her* eyes are not particularly beautiful, but at least they haven't started to slide down to her Adam's apple, like the rest of her face. And that color! Totally wrong for her. There's no use even saying anything about the style. What was Freddie trying to do, draping that poor woman in Julius Caesar's shroud? Somebody should report him to the A.S.P.C.A. Look at that bare arm. It looks like the beach after the hurricane."

I peeked at the woman in the photograph; her arms did have ripples, like sand after the tide has gone out.

"Well, it's her choice," my father said. "I pity her, and that is all I feel."

I agreed with Annette. Trying to sell things we had made wouldn't be my favorite work, either.

"We'll have to check this book out and finish reading it later," Annette said. "It's time for my lesson."

Every Saturday Annette's mother drives her out to a farm where a woman named Pat Hardy is teaching her to ride. "Pat is my mother's second cousin twice removed," Annette told me, "so she doesn't charge me." Everybody in Meterboro is the cousin of somebody else in Meterboro, except my mother and me. "Maybe Pat would teach you, too."

I could see my moon-colored horse galloping over the sagebrush with me on his back. My fair, wavy tresses would stream out behind me, and the cowboys and Indians would look up from their campfires and shake their heads at how fast my horse and I were flying and how beautiful my hair was.

In the mirror, my hair is brown and totally straight and short. Every so often my father will sit down to breakfast and say, "How's my Lhasa apso this morning?" (A Lhasa apso is a kind of dog that has bangs that totally cover its face. Nobody had one at the library pet contest, but there are several in New York.) Then my mother will notice my hair, and after school she will trim it.

Annette's mother braids Annette's hair every morning. When Annette unbraids her hair it is down to her elbows. I suggested to my mother that I might look more grown-up with braids, and she said, "Fine, if you are grown-up enough to braid them yourself. I don't have time." My mother doesn't care how I look as much as she cares how her pictures look.

When Annette and Mrs. Frazier and I got to the farm lane, I jumped out of the car and opened the big hollow-metal gate and then closed it again behind the car. "Be sure to fasten it," Mrs. Frazier said.

When I got back in the car, Annette said, "That gate has to stay closed, because if a horse ever got loose and ran out onto the road, it might get so excited that even if a car didn't hit it, it would run itself to death. I don't mind fastening the gate when the weather's like now, but sometimes in January ice freezes in the latch so it won't open till I take off my glove and thaw it with my bare hand."

The lane we were on led between fenced pastures straight to a barn and then curved, past a weeping willow with a pond underneath, toward a white house. Annette's cousin Pat was waiting for us in a paddock behind the barn, where she had set up cavalletti for Annette to jump her mare over. Cavalletti are wooden rungs placed in two wooden Xs; they look sort of like this:✕——✕. Annette can jump foot-high cavalletti.

Mrs. Frazier waved to Pat and let us out and drove on over to the house to talk to Mrs. Hardy.

Pat Hardy must be at least twenty-five. Her hair isn't black like Annette's but brown like mine, and even shorter than mine. She had on boots and jodhpurs and an open-necked tan shirt and didn't look so bad, but up close I saw that her fingernails were not very clean. "This is my friend Sarah," Annette told her. "She comes from New York City."

"Hi, Sarah," said Pat. "Do you ride?"

I admitted that I didn't.

"Mmm," she said. "New York City, huh? Never been there myself. Shoot. Lexington's enough city for me. Anything bigger is a can of worms. Well, Nette, Chilly's waitin' for you."

Chilly is what everybody calls Windchill Factor, which is Pat's chestnut mare. I knew how much Annette loved her when she told me that the funny white splotch on Chilly's forehead is a star.

We all went in the barn, and Pat led Chilly out of her stall for Annette to saddle. I had never been that close to a horse before. From up close, Chilly's back looked as far off the ground as my bedroom window. "Maybe Chilly would let Sarah walk her around the paddock once first, Cousin Pat," Annette suggested.

She meant I would be sitting in the saddle.

"How about it, City-girl?" Pat asked me. "You might not be too old to learn something."

Chilly was looking at me sideways. "Maybe she'd rather get to know me first," I said. "She looks suspicious of me."

"She has to turn her head like that to see you at all, City-girl. Horses have to look at things with one eye at a time. Chilly can't look at you very well even with just one eye, when you're close to her like this." I took a step backward. "Horses can see a dog hiding the far side of the pasture better than they can see the person putting a saddle on them. The best way to let Chilly get to know you is to get on her back. A horse always knows the quality of what's on its back; it'll respect you, if you know what you're doing."

I knew what I was doing; I was staying on the ground. "I don't think my dentist would like me riding horses," I said. "He wants my teeth to last another eighty years."

Pat laughed. "You sound just like my cousin Harlan Bedford. He wouldn't be your dentist, would he?" I hadn't meant to *sound* like Dr. Bedford. "Don't you worry about Cousin Harlan. If Chilly throws you, it won't be your mouth that's sore." She laughed again, but I was sure she couldn't be sure.

"I'd rather not ride today," I said. I knew I sounded like those women who tell Annette they're looking for pink pots. I wished I had never come to Kentucky.

"You'd rather not ride tomorrow, either, wouldn't you, City-girl?"

Annette looked anxious. I knew she wanted Pat and me to like each other. "Chilly won't go any faster than you tell her to go," she coaxed me. "She has a very gentle mouth."

Chilly had drawn her lips back off her teeth. She has a mouth like an alligator.

"Never put a chicken on a horse," Pat told Annette. "You don't know when it will start squawking and spook the horse. And that's when a good horse can get hurt." She joined her hands together and Annette put her left knee in them and jumped onto Chilly's back.

I hated Pat Hardy totally. Her fingernails were black and she smelled like sweat. I decided I would never come back to that farm, and I wouldn't watch Annette's lesson right then, either. I had seen some ducks land on the pond under the willow tree. I walked over there to see what kind they were.

Behind me Pat was yelling, "Light, I want to see light under those knees!"

There were two male ducks and two females. Their breasts looked like speckled eggs and they had beautiful pale blue patches on their wings. They quacked and peeped very quietly to each other and swam close together. Their ripples flowed out around them like magic circles, keeping them safe. "High, high!" I could hear Pat yelling at Annette. "Get those wrists high!" I stayed watching the ducks until Annette climbed down.

I thought Annette would be mad with me for not watching her, but she acted as if nothing had happened. (Actually, I did watch her a little, when Pat's back was turned. Annette says she loves riding, but the reason she loves to ride didn't show, at least not to me.) Annette met me with a big smile. "We've got a job!" she said. "Pat says Saturday is her barn man's day off, and she'll pay us a dollar-fifty an hour apiece every Saturday to muck stalls!"

I saw Pat sneak a look at me. I didn't know what "muck stalls" meant, but I understood "every Saturday." I opened my mouth to say I'd have to ask my mother. My mother isn't perfect, but she never gives me permission to do things when I ask her not to.

"That's if they're not allergic to hard work in New York City," Pat said. I shut my mouth.

"A dollar and a half an hour is all Lulu's sitter gets," Annette told me. We had already admitted to each other that neither of our mothers realizes we are old enough to baby-sit. "Isn't Pat a doll?"

Pat laughed, and we all went in the barn. Pat got a couple of pitchforks and leaned one against the wall while she demonstrated how to throw dry bedding into the stall corners and the dirty straw and manure piles into the muck bucket. Muck is manure. Some was hard and some was sploshy. Pat acted as if Annette were my mother and there wasn't any need or use telling me anything personally. After she finished telling Annette everything, she stuck her pitchfork handle at us. Since she'd been sort of ignoring me, I thought she meant for Annette to take it, and for me to get the other one, so I didn't move right away. "Don't be afraid of it, City-girl," Pat said, jiggling the handle. "It's not a horse." I wanted to throw the first forkful right down her open-necked shirt. Maybe it's lucky she turned her back on me again. "I'll tell your mother you'll be a little late, Nette," she said. "Next week, she can just drop you off, and I'll take you home." So I was going to have to ride in her car besides. My father will never know what I went through to buy him a Christmas present.

In a shed behind the barn was a tractor attached to a long wagon. Before she left, Pat drove this into the barn, and I saw that the wagon bottom was a row of scary-looking blades. "That's a manure spreader," Annette said. "Once it's full, the barn man drives it round and round an empty pasture with the blades turning. The muck gets chopped up and falls through the blades and makes an even layer of fertilizer on the pasture."

Our job was to put the pitchfork tines under just enough of the straw beneath each manure pile to be able to lift the pile into the spreader. Too little straw, and pieces of the hard manure would roll off the fork or wetness from the sploshy manure would be left behind to attract flies. Taking too *much* straw is wasteful. One bale of straw costs as much as a movie ticket, Annette says.

Chilly's manure doesn't stink as bad as my cousin's dog's, but she makes a lot more of it.

6

Horizons

The Tuesday after I got a blister mucking my first stall, I got another job. A blind friend of Mrs. Hume's who lives at the other end of Simon Kenton Street from me likes to be read to. Mrs. Hume told us about each other; that's how I got the job.

Every time I talked to my mother about my father, she started frowning, and if I kept on talking, she asked me if I'd finished my homework; so when I asked her if I could read to Mrs. DeMeter, I told her I wanted to earn money to buy something for Annette's birthday. I wasn't fibbing, because I had decided that I would get Annette something for her birthday and for Christmas, too. Just not my mother. "Annette's birthday is right after Thanksgiving," I said.

My mother pulled in the sides of her mouth. "I wish you could have an allowance the way you did in New York, but I don't know what it costs to heat this house come winter, and I have to make what my publisher gave me last till I finish this job and he pays me the rest." Then she gave a little shrug and went back to her easel.

So: We aren't going to be home for Christmas, and she knows it. Why didn't she tell me so? When somebody asks you when she can go *home,* telling her "We'll see" is about as useful as saying "It will be well before you're married" to somebody who is throwing up.

She did give me permission to go to Mrs. DeMeter's house every school day, even before I do my homework, and read aloud for one hour. Mrs. DeMeter pays me a dollar-fifty. She has a special money holder with dividers in it so she knows where each kind of money is, and she has never given me the wrong change yet.

The trees around Mrs. DeMeter's house are huge. That's how you know the house is old. Mrs. DeMeter told me it was a wedding present from her great-grandfather to her grandparents, and she was born in it. The doorbell looks like a doorknob, but you don't turn it, you pull it in and out. A bell rings inside, and Mrs. Kenrick, the woman who lives with Mrs. DeMeter, comes to the door. Most people wouldn't know the knob was a bell, but Mrs. Hume had told me about it. I have to get Mrs. Hume a Christmas present, too.

Mrs. Kenrick wears crepe and pink plastic-framed glasses and has red hair, except close to her head. "I'm going to read to Mrs. DeMeter," I told her.

"You are?" she answered with an extra-bright smile, the way you might if Lulu told you she was going to help Mrs. Frazier fix supper.

"Come in, Sarah," I heard someone call from the first room off the hall where Mrs. Kenrick was standing, and Mrs. Kenrick lost that smile and followed me into the front parlor, where Mrs. DeMeter was sitting under the portraits of her ancestors. "Thank you, Kenny," Mrs. DeMeter said.

Mrs. Kenrick looked a little anxious and not really pleased. "Your book is right there on the table," she said, "and—"

"I know where my book is, thank you, Kenny." Mrs. DeMeter put her hand on the book on the little table beside her chair, and Mrs. Kenrick went away.

I wish Mrs. DeMeter could see herself, because she is beautiful. She has wavy white hair and it always stays neat because she wears a hair net, although you can't see that until you are close, because it is made of her own hair. She sits very straight, like Annette on Chilly.

I think what Mrs. DeMeter most misses seeing is Kentucky, because I've noticed that her favorite books are the ones by Kentuckians that tell her how beautiful it is, whether they are stories or poems. Most of the poems don't rhyme, but Mrs. DeMeter doesn't care, just so they remind her what Kentucky looks like. I think it must be awfully sad to be blind, but Mrs. DeMeter says not to mind, that unheard melodies are sweeter.

I always feel I ought to say something when Mrs. DeMeter tells me anything, because otherwise she might think I have tiptoed away and left her alone, but sometimes I don't know what to say. When she said that about unheard melodies, I started to answer "I see," but I stopped, not just because I actually didn't understand at all, but because I didn't want to say "I *see*" to Mrs. DeMeter.

"You look unconvinced," she said.

I am not surprised anymore when Mrs. DeMeter says "look" for "sound." I think she believes it relaxes people if she pretends she can look. Or else she thinks it keeps us on our toes. If I were blind I would always be wondering if the people talking to me were making faces at me, the way I sometimes do at my mother after her back is turned.

"I think the poet who wrote that meant something like what you told me about your mother's silhouette princess," Mrs.

DeMeter said. "The one everybody likes best because your mother didn't draw her profile, so everybody imagines her to suit himself. It's not just what something looks like that might be better if we imagined it, or remembered it. Which are very often the same things," she added. "Do your New York friends seem nicer to you now than they did when you could be with them anytime?"

"Um," I answered.

"Do you find yourself thinking they were more agreeable to you than your Meterboro friends?"

"*Nobody* is more agreeable to me than Annette Frazier."

"Good. Good for you, Sarah. That shows unusual maturity. Most of us tend to see the faults of the people we're rubbing up against every day, and to remember just the best things about the ones we can't be with anymore."

"I am not like that," I said.

When I got home, Dr. Bedford was there to remind my mother that I had a dental appointment the next day. Usually his secretary telephones and reminds people, but my mother and I cannot afford a telephone in Meterboro. If we had one, Dr. Bedford would not have to come here, and also I could telephone my father.

Dr. Bedford was interested in my job. "DeMeter is a very good name in central Kentucky," he told my mother and me. "It's a known fact that Mrs. DeMeter's husband's great-great-grandfather had the first mill in this county. Meterboro was named for him."

My mother was making Dr. Bedford a cup of coffee. "Would you like some milk?" she asked me.

"I have to do my homework," I excused myself, and went upstairs.

I like my teacher this year, Mrs. Berryman. She lets me sit right across the aisle from Annette even though we are best friends. Miss Sanchez never let best friends sit together. When everybody had to have a science project, Annette and I were partners. Our project was Annette's idea. It wasn't messy or scary, and everybody said it was the best one. We took a tall glass of water and put two tablespoons of vinegar and one teaspoon of baking soda in it, and quick while it was fizzing, we dropped in mothballs. Every few minutes the mothballs would rise in the glass and then fall, and Annette explained what this proved about the things we had put in the glass reacting to form carbon dioxide. We both got an *A*. I began to think maybe fourth grade would be a thousand times better than third grade, and right away, something terrible happened.

In third grade, I won every single spelling match, so I wasn't surprised when I and another girl, Sue Lyn Mefford, were the last ones standing in the first spelling match in Mrs. Berryman's class. I had seen Sue Lyn at the library contest; she had brought a woolly dog. "I call my dog an Afghan hound," she had said, "because she lies on the bed."

When I saw that the spelling-match winner would be either Sue Lyn or me, I told myself that if I won, my mother would take me home by Easter, but if I lost, we would never go home. Then I really concentrated!

When my word came I was so tense thinking how important it was not to lose that I didn't notice I wasn't saying the letters the way I meant to. Mrs. Berryman gave me a second chance. "Hor-i-zons," she said, extra plainly. I knew she thought I should slow down and think. I felt cold all over because I was sure I had spelled it right, H, O, R, I, Z, O, N, S, and I couldn't think how else to spell it. Could there be two Rs? No: Two Rs would make the O like the O in holly, and Mrs. Berryman was saying HO as in horse. I heard my voice get high when I tried again, but I spelled very slowly, in case Mrs. Berryman just hadn't heard me right the first time. Mrs. Berryman shook her head and turned to Sue Lyn, and Sue Lyn said "Horizons, H, O, R, I, Z, O, N, S."

"That's what I *said*," I protested. "That's what *I* said."

"You said 'H, R, O,' " Mrs. Berryman told me. She looked sympathetic, as if she knew it was just a flub-up, but Sue Lyn was smiling, and I felt as if somebody was pouring hot water down my freezing back. I stumbled back to my desk and thumped down in my seat.

"Don't cry," Annette whispered, which made me furious, because I have never cried in class.

I have just got to think of some way to make my mother want to be with my father as much as I do.

7

Fight, Fight, Fight for the Blue and White

Saturday I had permission to spend the day with Annette again. "I've been looking through the rest of *Forty Ways to Buy a Sled*," she said as she let me in the house. "Can you sing?"

"Not very well," I admitted. (The music teacher at home told me that she didn't think I could hit a high note if she tied me to the chandelier by my hair.) "Why?"

Annette stuck *Forty Ways* at me, open to a page that said "GIVE A CONCERT!" and, of course, "Charge admission!"

The illustration was six kids playing paper-wrapped combs. "I can play a comb," I said.

"We can do better than that," Annette answered. "Come look what I've got on the back porch." On the back porch was a small hand organ. "I asked Simms if I could play his accordion this morning," Annette explained, "and he said yes. I can play, and you can collect money."

"How will anybody know to come hear us?" I asked. "Who would guess we were all of a sudden going to give an accordion concert?" At least she hadn't said any more about me singing!

"I wasn't thinking about our having a concert on the back porch," Annette said. "I was thinking about our standing on the busiest corner on Main Street. Simms has taught me how to play only one song, but I know the words, and they're easy. You could learn them in no time."

"Maybe I could learn to whisper them in no time," I said. "Singing is something else."

Annette just smiled. I could see her thinking, Sarah is modest and nervous, but when she relaxes she will sing okay. "It's not a hard tune," she said. She began to sing:

"On, on, U of K, we are right for the fight today.
Hold that ball and hit that line; every Wildcat star
will shine.
We'll fight, fight, fight for the blue and white, as
we roll to that goal, varsity.
And we'll kick, pass and run till the battle is won
and we'll bring home the victory.

You sing it with me this time."

"I don't know it yet," I stalled.

"This time I'll play it, too," said Annette, and began to pump up the accordion. One hand just went *boom, drip drip, boom, drip drip* the whole time, and the other sort of groaned out the tune. "I'm still learning," Annette said.

She had sounded fine when she was just singing; but the trouble was, she couldn't play and sing at the same time. Everytime she tried, her hands would slow down. Then she would sing slower, to match her hands, but they would just slow down some more. My cousin's weimaraner would have thrown back his head and howled, she sounded that sad. "I think it will be better if I just play, and let you do all the singing," Annette said.

44

The trouble was, she couldn't listen to me try to sing without getting the giggles, and then her hands would quit completely, both the *boom, drip drip* and the tune. "I warned you!" I reminded her. Her giggling made me giggle. "I have a better idea," I finally told her. "Let's take shoe polish and paint my face like a monkey's. Instead of singing, I'll make monkey noises and shake a cup at people, the way organ grinder monkeys do."

"Oh, Sarah, that is dazz," said Annette. "You won't even need to paint your face, either. I've got a monkey mask from last Halloween."

I was a little disappointed to hear that, but Annette dug around in her bureau till she came up with a painted fabric monkey mask. The elastic cord had pulled off of one side, but Annette fastened a big safety pin to the fabric and tied the cord to that and it wasn't too uncomfortable. If we had been in New York, my father would have given us some red cloth and stuff. I could have had a red jacket with braid like the organ grinder's monkey that collects money in the park near our apartment. Instead I was wearing my MOMA T-shirt. (MOMA doesn't stand for your mother; it stands for Museum of Modern Art. I got my T-shirt last year when an old professor of my mother's had a private show there, and my mother took me. The MOMA has *some* pictures of real things you can recognize, like angels; it even has some by that French painter who is my mother's favorite, Degas, but I didn't get to see any of them that day. I had to stay at the reception with my mother and pretend to like her professor's smears and drippings. The T-shirt was my consolation prize, my mother said.)

My father would have given us some fake fur for a tail, too. As it was, Annette took the belt out of the loops of her bathrobe and knotted one end to my belt. I would have liked to ram some wire in it so we could make it stick up and curl, but there wasn't any in the garage, and we couldn't think where else to look, and Simms and Mr. and Mrs. Frazier weren't home to ask. "Did you tell Simms why you wanted to play his accordion?" I asked Annette.

"He didn't ask," she said. "Let's go."

Saturday morning is very busy on Main Street in Meterboro. Lots of people were walking and driving by the corner Annette and I chose. A few frowned and a few stared and a few wouldn't look our way, but most looked at us and laughed. Even the friendly laughers, though, didn't give us any money. "We should have pinned signs to our shirtfronts," Annette said.

"The monkey that does my job at home rattles his cup," I told her. "He always has a couple of quarters at least in it, so people will know that's what he hopes they'll give him."

I didn't have any money, but Annette had a dime and a penny. She dropped them in my can (I was using an empty soup can for a cup because all the Fraziers' cups are pottery) and I began rattling them and jumping around the way a monkey does. It worked! Mostly we got pennies, but once in a while a nickel. Whenever anybody put anything in the can, I would *cheep-cheep* very excitedly. The more money was put in, the faster and higher and more I would cheep. When one man gave us a quarter, my cheeps would have surprised my music teacher. Just then the grocer whose store we'd been performing in front of came out. I hopped over to him, rattling my can. He looked at me and shook his head. He must not have been able to tell if I was a boy or a girl, because he turned to Annette and said, "Little lady, my customers haven't complained about your music, but they get to fill their bags and leave. That's one of my favorite songs you're playing, but there is a limit to how many times in a row I want to hear it played on a hand organ. Now, I have just come out here to ask you kindly, either choose another tune or choose another corner."

"It's the only tune I know," Annette said. "We'll go across the street."

The WALK light was on, so we went right away. The grocer hadn't sounded mad, so I didn't think there was any harm in it when Annette stopped just as we stepped off the curb and played "On, On, U of K" to the man sitting in the first of the cars that were stopped at the red light. Two things were wrong with it. The first was that the grocer clapped his hands over his ears, made a terrible face, and went back in his store. The second was that the car driver was Dr. Bedford. He looked at us as if we were sitting across from him at supper picking our noses. I was glad I had on Annette's mask! I took hold of Annette's elbow and got her to come on. The light changed, Dr. Bedford drove away, and we began to collect pennies in front of the S & S Sundry Store.

I don't think we'd collected more than about twenty more pennies when I saw Dr. Bedford coming back—this time, with my mother. I hated to see that, but I would have hated it more if I had realized they weren't just going somewhere but were headed straight for us.

When the car got to our corner, my mother rolled down her window and said to Annette, "Sarah has to come home now. Would you like a ride to your house?"

All the way to Annette's corner, nobody said one word. As the car began the curve, I started to give Annette our money can, but either my mother has eyes under her hair or she saw me in the mirror. "Better give me that for now, Sarah," she said.

That was all till Annette was about to get out. "Call me," she whispered. Then she remembered that my mother and I don't have a telephone, and she looked even sicker.

When we got to our house, my mother didn't ask Dr. Bedford in. "Thank you, Harlan," she said. He looked at me as if I didn't have the kind of mouth he would ever want to put his fingers in again, which if you'd asked me I would have said was okay with me, but for some reason I still hated to be looked at that way.

My mother and I went inside and sat down. Here's what Dr. Bedford had told her about Annette and me. We were playing in the middle of the street, interfering with traffic, begging, making respectable merchants so furious they were driving us from door to door—

Here's what my mother and I agreed to after I told my side. *Forty Ways to Buy a Sled* would go back to the library immediately. I would check any further plans for collecting money with my mother first. Annette should get her dime and penny back, but the rest of the money in the can she and I would take to the store of the grocer we had bothered and put every coin of it in the muscular dystrophy collection box on his counter.

"It's a long walk to Main Street," I mentioned.

"I'm sure Mrs. Frazier will drive you after I've talked to her," my mother answered. "You can stop on your way to the Hardys'." She'd said I could go ahead and spend the afternoon with Annette because we had promised Pat, and a legitimate job is a duty. Her voice underlined *legitimate*.

Annette and I waited to talk about it all till we were alone with our pitchforks. "How did he know it was me?" I demanded. "The grocer didn't even know if I was a girl or a boy!"

"I bet it was your T-shirt," Annette said.

So! That T-shirt had been the only thing I had liked about my last trip to the MOMA, and now I didn't like that, either.

8

Demeter

Telling my father about Mrs. DeMeter filled both sides of my page, so I saved my barn job for another letter.

"Demeter," my father wrote back, "was the Greek goddess who made things grow—flowers and trees and crops and all—until she was separated from her daughter. Then in her grief she brought the earth no sunshine. No leaf uncurled and no flower bloomed, no apple reddened or grape purpled, the grass all turned brown and all the streams froze, and the other gods saw there would be no life left on earth if Demeter went on grieving for her daughter. They made arrangements that let the girl spend some months each year in her old home, and some in her new home, and that made all the difference to Demeter.

"Winter, the Greeks said, was the months Demeter didn't have her daughter with her, and spring and summer and fall were the months when she did."

"Would you grieve," I asked my mother, "if I didn't live with you all year?"

"What has your father been writing you?" my mother asked me.

I asked Mrs. DeMeter if she knew the story of Demeter. "Yes," she said. "I've always thought she was childish and selfish. People shouldn't spoil things for everybody just because they're unhappy themselves."

"But if she hadn't," I said, "the gods wouldn't have paid any attention, and her daughter didn't like being dragged off like that one bit. I think Demeter was a good mother."

"Children have to grow up and leave home sometime," Mrs. DeMeter said. "Parents who don't teach them that aren't good parents."

I wished my father could arrange to make it so cold in Kentucky that the horses my mother is drawing couldn't leave their barns, and she would have to go back to New York. Mrs. DeMeter doesn't understand how families feel when they are separated, I thought, because she has never been dragged off. She has always lived right here in Meterboro.

"Do you like mythology?" she asked me. "Let's read some. Look on the shelves just left of the Confederate soldier and choose a book."

She meant the portrait of the Confederate soldier. He looks younger than my father, but he was her grandfather. I found books of myths from practically every country. "What country do you want?" I asked her.

"Oh, let's read our own ancestors' stories today," she said. "Look for a book called *In the Morning of Time*."

I found it. "It says on the cover these are Norse legends," I said. "My ancestors were English."

"Lots of Vikings settled in England," said Mrs. DeMeter. "The Vikings were Norsemen. Read me about Skadi."

Here is what I read. All the Norse gods lived on a mountaintop, and the top god was Odin. Skadi was a lonely orphan. She was not a goddess, but because she was so beautiful, Odin promised her a god for a husband. That made Skadi happy, because she thought life on the mountaintop would be a ball, but the husband Odin gave her was Njord, the one god who lived far below the mountain, beside the cold sea. His duty was to calm the sea when it was stormy. Skadi said she could never live in that foggy harbor with nobody around but Njord, never, and Njord said he had to live where his work was and that was that, but Odin suggested a compromise. They should take turns, nine nights on the mountaintop, then nine in the harbor, and so on.

Njord tried just nine nights on the mountaintop and said he would not go back. "The wailing of wolves seemed ill after the song of swans," he said.

Skadi was even worse. She spent only three nights in Njord's harbor before she came crying back to Odin. She couldn't sleep there, couldn't ever sleep there, she told him, for the crying of the waterfowl. She stayed on the mountaintop from then on and became the snow goddess, which I don't think was fair, because she broke her promise to Njord. "I think if a husband's work makes him stay in a certain place, his wife should stay with him," I told Mrs. DeMeter. "I don't like Skadi one bit."

"Well, I think that's the ideal way, Sarah," she said, "but why do you blame only Skadi? Lots of husbands sleep one place and go off to work somewhere else every morning." My father does that, but I didn't say anything. I have never talked to Mrs. DeMeter about my father.

"I can't blame Njord for not wanting to commute," Mrs. DeMeter said, "but do you think he tried hard enough to make Skadi like his harbor? Maybe if he had given her some ducklings to take care of, she would have learned to like waterfowl. My father used to say, you catch more flies with honey than with lectures."

Then she started telling me about her ancestors, who all came from places the Vikings went, she says, like France, and she asked me about mine, but not nosy questions. I don't think she ought to pay me for time I spend talking instead of reading aloud, but she has a special watch she reads with her fingers, and she always knows when I am supposed go home. "Time for you to do your studying, Sarah," she'll say, or, "Time for you to pose for your mother. I'll see you to the door." Mrs. DeMeter knows how many steps there are between her chair and every other place in her house she likes to go. She always walks me to the front door.

Once as she stood up, I thought I should tell her that she had a loose shoelace, because I was afraid she would trip. "I'll tie it for you," I offered.

"Thank you, I will do it," she said. She didn't tie it as fast as I would have, but when she finished she smiled at me and said, "Sometimes what's more important than the jobs themselves is that people do the jobs for themselves."

9
Frog-boy

"Hey, look out," somebody had yelled just as Annette and I got to school the first day. "Here comes the Dragon Lady!" A bunch of kids were chasing a dog that had a stick they seemed to think they had to have, but they quit and looked at us. I recognized the one who had yelled; he was the boy who had brought his frog to the library pet contest. "If you put a frog in the refrigerator, he doesn't die," this boy told everybody that day; "he just goes to sleep." Now he had his hands up in front of his face as if he had to protect himself from me. His shoulders were all hunched as if he were scared to death. "Watch out for the Dragon Lady!" he screamed.

I was glad Annette was with me. "Hi, Frog-boy," I said, and Annette and I walked on by.

"Oooh!" we heard Frog-boy moaning in a scared voice. We didn't look back.

Frog-boy turned out to be Australia J. Caywood, and he is in our class. Frog-boy's father is the Reverend James S. Caywood of the Meterboro Primitive Baptist Church. Mrs. Caywood named Frog-boy Australia, he says, because she always hoped the church would send her husband to a mission in Australia, but Frog-boy says they have never sent him anywhere outside Kentucky.

Maybe his mother's wanting to travel is why suitcases are on Frog-boy's brain. (Australia sounds like a girl. I never call Frog-boy *Australia*.) He pretends to think my lunchbox is a suitcase. A lot of the kids go home for lunch—Annette does—but my mother doesn't like to have her concentration broken. "I'm like a car," she says. "Every time I have to start my engine, I have to warm up for a while before I can get anywhere—so it isn't just the time I would spend fixing your lunch, Sarah, it's the time I would lose warming up to the job again after you left." Some of the kids go to the cafeteria, but I would have to pay, so I take my lunch. A lot of us do—Frog-boy does—but I'm the only one who has a box. The others all use paper bags.

The first time Frog-boy saw my lunchbox he said, "What's *that*, Dragon Lady?" When I told him, he laughed. "Dragon Lady flew all the way from Noo Yawk with her suitcase," he told everybody. He said New York as if I were about thirty years old and really snooty, which I am not. "What's that on the side, your claw print?"

"That's my monogram," I told him. "My mother designed it and painted it there for me. She's an artist."

Frog-boy's voice got even higher, and he stuck one hip way out and put his hand on the other like my father's models. "Mah mothah's an ah-teest!" he mimicked. "She painted me mah *mumble*-gum on mah *soot*-case." After that when he saw Annette and me coming down Henry Clay Street in the morning, Frog-boy always called out, "Hey, watch out, everybody! Here comes Dragon Lady with her Noo Yawk mumble-gum soot-case!"

54

My mother gave me my lunchbox, so I didn't want to tell her that everybody was laughing at it. Instead I just mentioned that paper bags are lighter. "People in fourth grade carry more books than smaller kids do," I pointed out. "Everybody else in my room just uses little grocery bags."

My mother got her money expression. "You and I make a very small family," she said. "I don't buy as many groceries as most of your classmates' mothers. I would have to buy bags extra, and that doesn't make sense, when you already have your nice box."

It *was* a nice box, for New York. Everybody in my third grade that brought lunch to school had a box, and a few kids had theirs initialed, but mine was the only one with a monogram.

One night my mother said, "Sarah, I have to leave before your breakfasttime tomorrow. I need to draw weanlings as they're led to pasture, and Dr. Bedford has offered to come by early and drive me to a big farm. Can you rinse your dishes and pack your own lunch and be sure to lock the door when you leave?"

"Sure," I said. "What's a weanling?" I asked her a question right away so she wouldn't start telling me what to pack.

A colt so old that he doesn't get to stay with his mother anymore ever again is called a weanling. (The little horses never do get to stay with their fathers, Annette says.)

My mother was right about not having many little grocery bags. In the morning I could find only one, and she was already using it to line the garbage can and it had eggshells and potato peels in it.

My mother's sandwiches were always made either with peanut butter, which I like, or leftovers, which I usually like. Chicken sandwiches are good, mackerel sandwiches are okay, bean sandwiches are boring, and so on. I wouldn't like the same lunch every day. Frog-boy always has ham biscuits, every single day. Sometimes he has an apple, but he always has ham biscuits. The morning Dr. Bedford drove my mother to that farm to see weanlings learning to be led without their mothers, I made peanut butter sandwiches for my lunch, but I added a thick layer of grape jelly. Dr. Bedford says children should never be given jelly sandwiches because it's a known fact that jelly causes cavities.

"Did you have a good lunch, Sarah?" my mother asked me that night.

"Totally," I said. She looked pleased.

The next day at breakfast my mother said, "I think yesterday's system was a good one. By fixing your own sandwiches you're sure to get something you like, fixed just the way you like it. No more beans, huh?" She smiled at me as if she were doing me a favor.

I fixed my lunch. I didn't put in even any peanut butter, just jelly, twice as thick as the day before.

"I'm taking the ten o'clock bus to Lexington," my mother told me, "because I've run out of charcoal fixative and I can't buy it in Meterboro—but I'll be back before you get home from Mrs. DeMeter's."

Halfway to school I realized that my box was empty. I had left my sandwiches on the kitchen counter. There wasn't time to go back. I couldn't even go home at lunch recess and eat because my mother wasn't going to be home, and I don't have my own key.

When I got to school I put my lunchbox on the coat-closet shelf the way I do every morning. (The kids who use bags can put their lunches in their desks, but my lunchbox is too big.) When recess came, Frog-boy noticed that I wasn't hurrying to the closet the way I usually do. "Don't you like what

you have in your mumble-gum suitcase today, Dragon Lady?"
he asked.

"Yes I do," I fibbed, and jumped up to get it. I could take
it to the girls' room with me, I thought, and stay awhile. When
I came back I could pretend I had eaten.

Frog-boy must have been fed up with ham and biscuits,
because he wasn't eating either. Instead he watched me get
my box and said, "Why are you carrying it like that? Are you
afraid your lunch will jump out at you? What have you got
in there, Dragon Lady?"

I wondered if his frog had jumped out of his refrigerator at
him. I realized that I was carrying my lunchbox close to me,
just as if I were afraid somebody would see right through the
lid that there was nothing inside. I had never let Frog-boy get
me mad before, but I was hungry, and I wasn't even going
home after school and eat like all the other kids, because I
had to read to Mrs. DeMeter. Things were hard enough without Frog-boy making them harder. "Come on, Dragon Lady,"
he said. "Tell us what you've got."

I held my box up in my hand like a fancy waiter in a grown-
ups' restaurant and answered, "I've got three T bone steak
sandwiches and two slices of coconut cake."

Frog-boy grabbed the box right out of my hand and held it
over his head where I couldn't reach it. Everybody in the room
stopped eating to laugh at Frog-boy teasing me. "Not even a
Dragon Lady can eat all that," he said. The more I grabbed
and yelled at him to give me my lunch, the more he danced
around laughing. "You're supposed to be a Dragon Lady, not
a hog lady," he said. "You should offer one little slice of coconut cake to your friend Frog-boy."

"You eat your own lunch!" I yelled. "You give me that!"
He didn't. He opened the box and looked in. My face was

burning. I felt plain sick. Frog-boy stopped laughing or even smiling and he snapped my lunchbox shut and gave it to me. I snatched it and ran to the girls' room and didn't come back till the end of recess. I saw Frog-boy noticing my eyes and turned my back.

I was glad Mrs. DeMeter couldn't see how red my eyes were. Her book was hard for me to read that afternoon, because they were so swollen from crying. I am never going back to that school, I thought, *never ever*.

When I finally got home my mother said, "Did you leave those sandwiches on the counter for my lunch, Sarah, or did you forget them?"

"Forgot them," I said. Why should I fix her lunch? Besides, I was starving. If she thought I had eaten and I had to start posing before I did get some food, I would faint.

"You poor lamb," my mother said, as if she cared. "I was afraid of that. I put them in the refrigerator for you." I figured next she would say something about cavities and jelly, but she said, "Why don't you eat them now? You must be starving." Maybe next she would say she was sorry she had dumped her job off on me, I thought. Maybe next she would say she would start fixing my lunch again. "I think we should change our morning schedule just a little," she said. "If I call you fifteen minutes earlier, you won't be so rushed and apt to forget something."

I waited till I had eaten the first sandwich before I answered. *Counting ten is good; eating a sandwich is better,* my father always said. "Or I could fix my lunch before I go to bed at night," I suggested.

After supper I made two peanut butter sandwiches. Then I got a frying pan, put a sieve on top of it like a lid, and made my dessert.

Frog-boy didn't yell at me when Annette and I got to school

58

next morning. He didn't seem to see me. He never looked my way once, till lunchtime. Then he said, "Want an apple, Dragon Lady? I've got two."

"Thank you," I said. "I was so busy fixing popcorn for my lunch today, I forgot to give myself any fruit."

He looked away, embarrassed. I could tell he thought I was fibbing again. I went to the closet and got my lunchbox and the shoebox I had put beside it. I had made enough popcorn for everybody to have some, and packed it in lots of little sandwich bags. I went down the aisle giving every kid who had brought his lunch a sandwich bag of popcorn. I gave Frog-boy two. "Because of the apple," I said. I didn't know if I could look at him, but I managed to smile.

Frog-boy stood up and said, "Step right up and get your popcorn, folks! No other popcorn like it! Made entirely without electricity! Dragon Lady just blows on the kernels with her fiery breath!"

I can't think of anybody else I ever knew who is like Frog-boy.

10

"My Name Is Rachel"

"Will you read me my mail, Sarah?" Mrs. DeMeter asked me. "Mrs. Kenrick tells me I have a letter from my son."

> *Sorry I missed visiting you on your birthday*, I read. *What with all this mission involves, I probably won't get to Meterboro this fall, either, but I'll telephone you on Thanksgiving.*
> *Be sure to have your radio on for the launching. I've never been asked any questions on the air, but my turn might come; you never know.*

"My son is an aeronautical engineer for NASA," Mrs. DeMeter explained. "He lives in Houston, Texas.

"You're interested in birds; maybe you'll go to Houston one day. That's where the whooping cranes spend the winter."

I hadn't known Mrs. DeMeter had a son. Houston is a long way from Meterboro . . . maybe as far as New York.

After I finished her mail, Mrs. DeMeter said, "Today, why

don't you read me something out of the book you're reading yourself? I think I'd like that."

I don't carry my library books back and forth to school; I might lose one. I was sure Mrs. DeMeter already knew everything in my schoolbooks. I opened my *Arithmetic Studies* and riffled the pages. "I don't have the story I'm reading with me," I said, "but I could read to you out of the magazine we get at school." Actually, I never bring that magazine home, because it's not worth carrying.

Mrs. DeMeter agreed to that, so I said, "The name of this story is "Home."

"*My name is Rachel,*" I began, using my read-aloud voice. "*My home is in Boston, but I do not live in Boston. My father does live there. My mother and I . . .*" I told Mrs. DeMeter about my father and mother and me, but I made my mother a writer and my father a dentist. I told what I knew and stopped.

"Are your eyes tired?" Mrs. DeMeter asked.

"No," I said, "that's all there is in this issue. It's a serial."

"I see," said Mrs. DeMeter. "Well, I think it's going to have a happy ending. It sounded to me like a story that will have a happy ending."

"What would Rachel do if you were writing the next chapter?"

"Rachel's mother and father are the ones who are going to decide where they'll live and where they'll work. Rachel can't tell them. In eight years, she will graduate from high school and have to decide where *she* is going to work. If I were Rachel, I would concentrate my thinking on that question." I didn't sigh very loud, but she must have heard me. "In the meantime," she said, "if Rachel wants her mother to go back to Boston, and her mother can't go back till that book is finished, maybe Rachel should take typing at school so she can help her mother copy the finished chapters. Or do anything else she can to speed that job along. I'm sure the story's author will be able to think of things."

I thought about the night before when I was up in my room reading *The Trumpet of the Swan* instead of my homework and told my mother I couldn't come down and let her draw me carrying a feed bucket because I hadn't finished my arithmetic problems.

Then Mrs. DeMeter and I heard the kitchen door open and Mrs. Kenrick come into the house, and Mrs. DeMeter felt her watch and said, "I see it's time you went home," and "saw" me to the front door, and Mrs. Kenrick came out in the hall and said, "Good-bye, Sarah," with her little laugh. She still smirks when I come to read to Mrs. DeMeter, sort of the way you laugh at the zoo when the chimpanzee rides a tricycle, but she is glad I come, because she gets to run errands while I am in the house. Annette says this ought to make my mother realize that I am old enough to baby-sit, but it hasn't yet.

Sometimes I think two jobs are enough, anyway. I am working twice as hard stall-mucking as I did the first time. "I'll go ahead and get started while you're riding," I told Annette the second Saturday, "so we'll be ready to go home sooner."

"Well—if you don't mind working while I'm having fun."

It didn't look or sound like fun to me. "How many times," I could hear Pat scolding, "have I got to tell you not to grip with the knees when you pull on the reins? Pull means *stop*. Grip means *go*. Get that through your head before you drive the mare crazy!"

I was working in the barn, instead of sitting on the fence watching Annette ride, just exactly so I would have to hear as little of Pat Hardy as possible. I hadn't put her in my Rachel story, because, I thought, what if she was Mrs. DeMeter's cousin, too, and Mrs. DeMeter recognized her? "You didn't tell me you were kin to Dr. Bedford," I had reproached Annette that day Pat called him Cousin Harlan.

"I'm not. Cousin Pat's father was Dr. Bedford's aunt's brother-in-law." I was confused. "Don't worry about it. Shoot," Annette said in Pat's voice, and laughed. "Meterboro families are a can of worms."

I worked hard, but when Annette and Pat brought Chilly back, Pat looked around and said, "Shoot, you're slow. You'll never make it at the track, City-girl."

"I'm never going to work at a racetrack," I said. "I'm going to be an aeronautical engineer." Pat laughed harder than ever.

"How can you stand the way she yells at you?" I asked Annette after Pat left.

"She's only trying to help me," Annette said. "I do things without knowing it, like clutching Chilly with my legs, which makes her speed up, when I'm scared and want her to whoa. If Pat didn't tell me I was doing that, I would never stop."

One reason I hadn't done as much as Pat thought I should have done is that the blister I'd raised the week before had popped and left a sore place. Until that Saturday the only time I'd had a pitchfork in my hands had been leaning on one for my mother to draw. I hadn't rushed right home and told her so, but much as I hate to pose, it is easier than stall-mucking. It also doesn't smell bad. "This stuff stinks," I mentioned to Annette.

"It doesn't stink as bad as Lulu's diapers," Annette said.

Lulu hasn't worn diapers in years. "Maybe you just don't remember."

"Pat says anybody who can stand the smell of sauerkraut can just as well muck stalls," said Annette. "She says that what a horse does to make manure out of grass is about what cooks do to make sauerkraut out of cabbage."

Personally, I have never liked sauerkraut.

When I got home I saw that my mother had put something on top of my schoolbooks in my bedroom. I was afraid it was one of her lists of things I have to do before I can do whatever it is she thinks I want to do:

(1) MAKE YOUR BED.
(2) PUT THE DIRTY SOCKS UNDER YOUR BED INTO THE LAUNDRY BASKET.
(3) PUT THE BOOK HIDDEN IN THE BATHROOM TOWEL CLOSET BACK ON YOUR BOOKSHELF.

And so on. It wasn't a list at all; it was a watercolor of Annette. This picture was not art or an illustration either one—it looked *exactly like* her. She was sitting on a horse, which my mother had never seen her do, but she got everything exactly right. I wonder if, some of those times I had to sit in a saddle on the sofa back, my mother was working on Annette's picture, and not just that book? She even made the horse a chestnut like Chilly! The horse was sideways to the person looking at the picture, so its forehead, where Chilly has a "star," didn't show, but Annette's face was turned to look back at the person looking at her. It was a beautiful picture.

I ran downstairs to hug my mother. She seemed pleased. "I can't give you money to buy Annette a birthday present," she said, "but do you think she would like this?"

"She'll love it," I said, "and I love you."

We hugged each other again. "Whoosh," said my mother. "I love you, too, but you smell like horse. Take a shower before you set the supper table."

I am going to have to divide my Christmas money five ways: some for my father, some for Annette, some for Mrs. Hume, some for Mrs. DeMeter, and some for my mother. I think I will give my mother fixative. I can get Annette's father to buy some for me; he goes to Lexington every week. Then my mother won't have to spend hours on the bus; she can spend them finishing her book.

I am standing stiller when she needs me to pose than I used to. It's not as hard as it used to be. I guess fourth-graders naturally have stronger muscles than third-graders.

11

My Brilliant, Worthwhile, Totally Dazz Idea

Annette will be a good mother. She just loves Lulu. She thinks everything Lulu does is interesting. Most of my friends in New York used to say they never were going to get married, but Annette says she is, as soon as she graduates from college and gets a job and saves enough money for a horse of her own. "Then I'm going to get married and have three babies just like Lulu," she says. She is always getting picture books at the library to take home and read to Lulu. When I'm there, I help her choose. That's how I got my brilliant idea.

Mrs. Hume would have said my idea was worthwhile. Annette would have said it was dazz. I told myself it was totally brilliant, and I didn't tell anybody else about it—not Mrs. Hume, not Annette, not even my father.

How I got my idea was, I noticed that on the dust jacket of every picture book Annette and I looked at, the publishers had their address. A lot of the pictures in these books weren't as good as my mother's. Those publishers should give their next job to her, I thought. I started doing some arithmetic.

Mrs. Hume has a big machine in the library that makes a copy of anything you put on it every time you drop in a dime. The post office will sell you a stamped envelope for 27¢. For four hours of reading to Mrs. DeMeter or mucking stalls I could send nine publishers a copy of a picture of my mother's with a letter to say that she would be back in New York very soon and they should give her a book to illustrate, and with a stamped envelope addressed to me, in case they wanted to tell me to have her come see them right away. That would cost $5.76 of the six dollars I would get for my four hours. "I know children would love my mother's pictures," I would put in my letter, "because I am a child, and I do."

I have three charcoal sketches that my mother drew of me in New York. I could hardly wait to get home and choose which I would send. In one I am patting a baby goat at the zoo. In another I am sitting on one of the stone lions in front of the public library, and in the third I am showing off a Chinese hat my father bought me when he took me to Chinatown. I put them side by side on my bed and tried to decide which one would make the publishers give my mother a book. In the end I decided to send copies of all three. That raised the price to 84¢ for every letter, so I only copied six publishers' addresses. I made six copies of each picture, I wrote six letters, and I went to the post office.

I knew I wouldn't get any answers for a week, because that's how long it takes my father to answer me. After a week, I began to try to be the one to bring the mail in. Our Meterboro house has a little metal basket nailed to the wall beside the front door. The mailman comes by about three-thirty and puts all the letters anybody has sent my mother and me into that basket. My mother is never in a hurry to get the mail the way I am. Sometimes even after I've brought it in, hers will just sit unopened on our kitchen counter for hours, even when it's a letter from my father. I have been getting a lot of mail, ever since Annette and I began to try to save money. I fill in all the blanks that come to "Boxholder" and "Resident" saying that someone at this address may already have won all the oil in Mexico, or at least a battery-operated wristwatch, and to find out which, the blanks should be filled in and returned. Sometimes they give you a stamp, but I have permission to use my mother's. I can tell my mother doesn't think I will ever win anything, but she says she wants to be supportive and nonjudgmental about my activities, as long as they are not life-threatening. For my brilliant idea, though, I bought stamped envelopes at the post office, because I thought if I took twelve of my mother's stamps all at once it might change her attitude.

That was in September. The meadowlarks were still singing on the Hardys' fences, but the days were getting cooler. That made the horses' stalls not smell so bad, or else I was getting used to it. Mucking was still hot work, though.

The last Saturday in September (I still hadn't heard from any of those publishers), Mrs. Frazier stopped the car at the Hardys' gate and told Annette and me, "Don't latch it behind me, because I'm just going to turn around at the barn and come right back." It was my turn, so I hopped out. A really dazz hawk flew up out of the oak tree halfway up the barn lane. I wanted to stop and watch him till he landed somewhere, but I knew Mrs. Frazier was in a hurry to leave and Annette was in a hurry to ride. I shoved the gate wide enough to lodge on the dirt so it wouldn't swing back and bump the car, and I hopped back in. The hawk was still flying over the pasture.

"You'll see hawks here more often when winter comes," Annette said. I didn't tell her that because of my brilliant idea

I might not be around for very much winter. I felt a little funny.

Pat had come to the front of the barn to speak to Mrs. Frazier. "Mother says, would you stop in for a minute, Cousin Lucy? She's fixing to paste up her snapshots and she wants you to help her identify some relatives."

Mrs. Frazier laughed. "You can't count on me to keep all those people straight," she said, but she drove on over to the house. Annette and Pat took Chilly to the paddock in back of the barn and I began mucking. After a while Pat was yelling as usual, so when I stepped out of the barn to cool off for a minute, I went out the front way. It was quieter there, and besides, the last time Pat had seen me leaning on the barn she'd said, "I thought you didn't like to waste time, City-girl." Not liking to waste time was the reason I'd given her for getting to work with my pitchfork instead of watching her boss Annette around.

I glanced around the corner at how Annette was doing and noticed that Pat had left the paddock gate open. (Later, after the accident, Pat said, "Nette and I left the gate open," but it was her fault. How could Annette close a gate from Chilly's back? What happened to Annette was Pat's fault.) I started to go close it for them.

Chilly must have seen the gap the same time I did, because before I'd taken two steps she sailed over the last jump and headed straight for it. I knew I'd never beat her there, and my whole body felt like electricity because I remembered that the road gate was open too. I ran that way instead. I ran the fastest I have ever run in my life.

Sure enough, I heard Chilly's hooves in the lane behind me and Annette crying, "Whoa! Whoa, Chilly! Whoa!" I thought I had enough head start to beat them if I just didn't trip. I *made* it—but the gate was stuck on the dirt. Tugging wouldn't budge it. I was sweating and screaming at the gate, and Chilly was pounding down the lane faster all the time. I couldn't believe what was happening. Then I thought of lifting up, and the least little lift freed the gate and I swung it shut with a slam and turned around.

Annette was lying face-down in the lane and Chilly was coming right at me. I could feel the way her chest would smash into mine; I could hear that steel gate ringing as my skull cracked against it. I remembered Pat's saying how a horse doesn't see you very well when he's up close. "Yahh!" I yelled at Chilly, and waved my arms like an umpire gone crazy. Chilly skidded to a stop.

Pat was running down the lane, but she wasn't close to Annette yet. One of Annette's legs was moving a little, but it was just *moving*; Annette wasn't getting up, and I was afraid Chilly would whirl around and run back right over her. I reached out and sneaked a hand under her chin and took hold of her halter. I held on as well as I could, but Chilly was snorting and arching her tail and throwing her head from side to side. I held on with both hands and she almost swung me off my feet.

Pat quit running when she saw me take hold of Chilly. "Didn't want to excite her," she explained to me later, "more than she already was." She walked to Annette pretty fast, though, and when she gave Annette a hand up I was so glad to see Annette standing, I wanted to cry. Then Pat hurried over and put a shank on Chilly. Annette followed her, slowly. "Well, City-girl," Pat said, "you saved this mare's life. If she'd got out on that road, she'd have run herself to death, and that's if a car didn't hit her first."

I was trying not to breathe as hard as Chilly, and not to back away from her now that Pat had her. Annette claims a horse can't bite me with a bit in its mouth, but I don't believe her. "I think we should change Chilly's name," I tried to joke, so I wouldn't seem scared. "From now on I think we should change Chilly to Chili." I pronounced chili the way Miss Sanchez does, "chee-lee," so Pat and Annette would know I meant something hot, not chilly.

Pat laughed and Annette tried to. "You all right now?" Pat asked her.

"Just *f i n e*," Annette said, stretching her mouth like a tragedy mask when she said *f i n e* and then kind of grinning.

"And what did you do?"

"Clutched and pulled," Annette said disgustedly.

"That's right," Pat said. "Ready? I'll lead her to the paddock for you." Annette nodded and Pat joined her hands, and Annette put her knee in them and swung onto Chilly's back! When Pat straightened, she saw me staring at her. "We're all crazy down here, City-girl," she said, "but not too crazy to be scared of breaking our necks. If Nette doesn't get right back on, she'll spend all the time, between now and when she does, wondering if she dares—and she might decide she didn't."

We walked back to the paddock together. I was closer to Chilly than I like to be, but I tried not to let it show. "You sure saved the day, City-girl," Pat told me. "When I saw you turn and run I thought you were heading for cover, which wouldn't have been such a bad thing. It was a few seconds before I thought of the road gate, and no way I could have beat Chilly to it. Have you thought about going out for track in junior high?"

It's true that when I watched the Olympics on our TV in New York, I noticed that the female gold-star runners had figures and short hair just like mine.

12
Angels Have Feathers

The first four days of October we had dreary rain, and on the fifth day Mrs. Berryman called in sick and we had a substitute teacher. She was even drearier. "I am Ms. Hatten, class," she told us. She had three rings on her left hand and three on her right. I passed Annette a note: *Think she's married?* She printed something underneath that and passed it back. I had just time to read *Can't guess* before Ms. Hatten said, "What is that, Sarah?" The note was in my hand. If she had said, "Give me that," I would have, but she didn't.

I dropped both my hands into my lap and started shredding. "Paper," I said politely.

"What kind of paper, Sarah?" Ms. Hatten asked, getting up and walking toward me. She still hadn't told me to give it to her.

I had finished shredding it. "Trash, I guess." Vernelle Stevens snickered.

Ms. Hatten stopped halfway down the aisle and turned toward the snicker. "What's funny, Vernelle?" she asked. Vernelle scowled at me and mumbled something. "Always speak distinctly, Vernelle," Ms. Hatten said. "Speech is the difference between persons and beasts."

Annette had frozen when Ms. Hatten had caught her passing our note, but now she sneaked a look at me out of the corner of her eye and I could guess she was hoping what I was hoping, that Ms. Hatten had forgotten about us. No such luck. "Let me see this 'trash' you and Annette were sharing, Sarah," she said next, standing where she was. "Maybe it would be more interesting to me than you think."

I obeyed at once. The note hadn't been very big, and I had balled up the scraps in my hand after I tore them, and my hands always sweat when I get nervous, such as when I think a teacher is going to read that I have been counting her rings. The whole handful looked like something a breeze blew out of an English sparrow's nest, and when I held it out to Ms. Hatten she looked at me the way cowboys look at rustlers. The skin under her eyes got dark and her voice changed and she said a lot of things to me that weren't so, like that I was sly and disrespectful and thought I was smart. I had to stand at my desk with the whole class staring at me while she said those things. "If that's the way they teach you to behave in New York, young lady, then you just better remember you're in Kentucky now."

I wondered how she knew I was from New York. I wondered if Mrs. Berryman had told her, or somebody in the principal's office, or somebody else, like maybe she went to Dr. Bedford, too. I wondered what else somebody had told her, and what she might say in front of the whole class about my father and mother working in different places. My family is none of her business, I thought. Teachers should mind their own business! All this fuss, just because I wondered if she was married.

She never had taken the scraps from my hand. Now she told me to put them in the wastebasket. I had to walk up to her desk in front of everyone, with her following behind me as if I were some animal she was shooing.

"And people who laugh at what isn't funny aren't any better than what they're laughing at," Ms. Hatten said behind me. "I'm talking to you, Vernelle."

I had to face the class and walk back to my desk. Vernelle said something to me under her breath as I passed her, but I was so embarrassed my ears were humming and I didn't hear what it was.

After that every time I looked up from my work, Ms. Hatten was watching me.

When recess came it was no help at all, because rain was pouring down harder than ever and we couldn't go out on the playground. I was sorry for Annette for having to walk home for lunch in that rain, but as things went, I wish she had invited me to go with her.

Those of us who had brought our lunches got to eat them in peace, because Ms. Hatten went to the cafeteria, but then she came back and announced that now we would have supervised play. I was hoping she would announce a spelling match so I would have a chance to beat Sue Lyn, but instead we played a game called Donkeys Have Feathers.

In Donkeys Have Feathers, whoever is It stands in front of the class and calls out that this, that, or the other thing has feathers. The rest of the class stand beside our desks and raise both hands if what It says is true, and keep them by our sides if not. Whenever It catches somebody raising hands for a false or keeping them lowered for a true statement, that somebody has to sit down. The last one standing is the next It.

We had played Donkeys Have Feathers the last time rain had kept us in. Frog-boy had been It first. He had gone too fast and jerked his own arms up and down like wild no matter what he was saying, and I got so excited and confused trying to keep up, I hadn't known what I was doing.

Next Sue Lyn had gone along in a monotone, naming every bird in the barnyard—"Geese have feathers; turkeys have feathers; hens . . ."—pumping her arms till she seemed like a robot, and then just as I was practically hypnotized she had said, "Chairs have feathers" in that same bored tone of voice. Six of us had had to sit down.

The day Ms. Hatten supervised us, George Toadvine got to be It first. He started off just like Sue Lyn. "Wrens have feathers," he said, lifting his arms about as eagerly as me when I'm having a halfway-finished dress pinned on me. "Robins have feathers," he said just the same way. "Ravens have feathers." If nobody else remembered Sue Lyn's strategy, I thought, I would win. "*Swallows* have feathers!" George cried in a gotcha voice, and I clutched my arms to my sides. Vernelle won that game.

Vernelle Stevens is taller even than Annette. She has bones everywhere, including her nose, which is big and pointy. She lives near the Hardys' farm. One of her six brothers mucks Pat's barn weekdays. All of them look just like Vernelle.

Annette says it's because of those brothers that every time you say anything to Vernelle she doesn't like she offers to fight. You never know what she isn't going to like, either. She enjoyed something on TV that Annette didn't enjoy. "Want to fight?" she asked Annette. She wants us all to play softball; I suggest jump rope. "Want to fight?" she asks me. I keep away from her.

Vernelle wasn't as tricky as Frog-boy or Sue Lyn or George, and I began to think I might win. I held my breath and promised myself about going home soon if I won (but I was careful not to say that if I lost we wouldn't ever go). Then I really paid attention.

Vernelle tried so hard her face got red, but I was cool. Half the class was sitting down before she said, "Rocks have feathers!" and I was in trouble. If I could have read how she was spelling rocks, I wouldn't have had any problem, but since I couldn't, I raised one hand and kept the other against my leg. "Do you mean birds or fish?" I asked her.

"Sit down, you raised your hand!" cried Vernelle. My heart started to beat a little faster. "How do we know whether she meant roc birds or rock-fish?" I asked Ms. Hatten.

"Birds or fish?" Vernelle said. "I mean *rocks*."

"Oh, Sarah, quit showing off," said Ms. Hatten. "Who in the class has ever heard of rocs but you? Besides, they don't exist."

"Does she have to sit down?" Vernelle demanded.

"Go on," said Ms. Hatten.

A lot of the kids who were already sitting down gave me dirty looks, but Vernelle went on. "Crows have feathers, Cows have feathers—R.B., you missed, Sue Lyn—See how the others sit down when they make mistakes?" she asked me.

"I didn't make a mistake," I told her politely. "You said rocks—"

"Oh, Sarah, don't try to start an argument," Ms. Hatten said. "Here in Kentucky we believe in being good sports."

"Does she have to sit down?" pressed Vernelle.

"Just let her go on," said Ms. Hatten, sighing as if I was hopeless or not worth bothering about or both.

"Pigs have feathers," Vernelle said. She was watching me and nobody else. "Angels have feathers." I raised my hands. Vernelle's arm seemed to grow like Pinocchio's nose when he lied. She stretched it so far it seemed as if her forefinger was about to mash my nose. "*Now* you have to sit down!" she crowed.

I stared at her. "You said angels have feathers, didn't you? I raised my hands."

"Ms. Hatten, don't she have to sit down? She raised both hands, everybody seen her—so don't say you didn't!"

"I know I did," I said patiently. "That was *right*."

"It won't neither!" shouted Vernelle, and Ms. Hatten told me to take my seat.

On one floor of the biggest art museum in New York—not the MOMA, the Metropolitan—there are probably more pictures of angels than of any other thing. Last year my father decided to base a collection on the wings of these different angels, and he took me along to make his sketches. His favorite angels were by an Italian monk who painted before Columbus. This monk gave his angels red feathers, blue feathers, green feathers, striped feathers—all in beautiful patterns. *My* favorite was painted by a Frenchman. It wore a red gown and the backs of its wings were like peacock tails, but their undersides glowed like red-gold clouds at sundown. You could light a fire with one of those feathers. In olden times, Mrs. Hume has told me, people wrote letters with goose quill pens. She didn't know how many of these goose feathers it would take to write a book, but probably a lot, she agreed. With just one of those feathers from that red-robed angel, I think you could write a whole encyclopedia, and never even sharpen the point.

"Why should I sit down?" I asked Ms. Hatten. "Angels *do* have feathers."

To hear the way the class gasped you would have thought I had said that angels had head lice. "That's blasphemy," Sue Lyn whispered.

"Want to fight?" demanded Vernelle.

"Sit *down*, Sarah," said Ms. Hatten. "You know very well angels don't have feathers."

"What are their wings made of, then?" I could hardly ask; I was choking. "They have wings, don't they?"

77

"They have wings, but not made of feathers," said Ms. Hatten. "They *look* like feathers, but they aren't, because feathers are earthly, and angels are divine." Nobody looked on my side, not even Frog-boy. I sat down.

"Nyah-hah, Miss New York City," said Vernelle.

I didn't tell my mother about it, because I was sure she would agree with me, and maybe she would say something to Ms. Hatten or Mrs. Berryman (although she never has taken up for me with any teacher yet). What I was afraid was that if she did say something to Ms. Hatten or Mrs. Berryman, they might tell her about the note Annette and I passed, and how I did the next worst thing to swallowing it. So instead of telling my mother, I wrote my father.

My father never knows when he should be serious. "Of course angels have feathers," he wrote back, "and when you draw them you must outline *every single feather* with a *firm black line*." Totally not funny.

13

Immediate Plans

In October I got one of my envelopes back from New York. I absolutely ran up the steps to my room and tore it open. There was a very little sheet of printed paper inside. "Dear Contributor," the printing said. "Thank you for your story. Although it has merit, we are sorry to say that it does not fit our immediate plans. The Editors." I was so mad and disappointed I felt as if I had been eating Mexican food—all hot inside and my head prickling. I tore the letter and the envelope into pieces my mother couldn't put back together, marched them downstairs and dropped them into the garbage can. I didn't care. There were five more publishers I had written.

The week after that I got another answer. This one was just a printed list titled "Guidelines for Authors." It told how many words should be in the stories writers sent them, and that only happy endings were wanted, and no violence, profanity, or talking animals.

Lulu loves talking animals. (So do I.)

I didn't care—I had written four other publishers—but the

next day I asked Mrs. DeMeter what she thought of talking animals.

"You mean like in *The Wind in the Willows* or *Watership Down* or *Alice in Wonderland* or *The Sword in the Stone*?"

"Or *The Trumpet of the Swan*," I said.

"One of my favorites. If I ever get to feeling sorry for myself, Louis inspires me." I didn't know Mrs. DeMeter ever felt sorry for herself! "Heroes like Louis remind us that we owe it to our self-respect to meet some challenges."

I thought about that. "Is getting on Pat Hardy's mare a challenge I owe it to my self-respect to meet?" I asked.

"Are you refusing to mount the mare because riding doesn't interest you, or because you're afraid?"

"Both. I thought I would be interested, but after I saw how scary it was, it started to seem boring, too. I don't think it seems boring because I'm scared, but maybe it does."

"Does your mother ride?"

"No, she doesn't."

"Does your father?"

"He doesn't, either."

"So it is obvious to you that it is perfectly possible to lead a happy life without riding horseback. It is not obvious to Pat Hardy. There hasn't been anybody in Pat's family in seven generations who has not ridden horseback."

"Did you ever ride?"

"Yes, before I lost my sight."

"Were you scared the first time?" I hoped she would say *Absolutely terrified*.

"I was only four, and I rode in front of my grandfather. I felt perfectly safe, because he was holding me. Pat's father taught her the same way. But I'll tell you a secret about Pat. She has never flown. She is absolutely terrified of getting on an airplane. She missed her own brother's wedding because she would have had to fly to San Francisco."

I was scared of flying to Kentucky, but not because I was scared of flying. I would get on an airplane tomorrow, if it would take me back to New York.

When I got home I did something that kept me awake that night and the next night and the next. I know I shouldn't read the letters my father writes my mother. She shouldn't leave them lying around on the kitchen table, either. Actually I only read one page. (That was all that was lying on the table.) I read it and read it again. After I had read it three times I put it back on the table where I'd found it and went upstairs to my room and lay down on the bed.

My father's letter began with some stuff about hot necktie colors (Red is hot this fall) and footwear trends. Next spring shoes will have a fresh, uncluttered look, my father wrote. Then he wrote, "I have been invited to do a Christmas show in Paris. Why don't you come with me? I know you have always wanted to see the Degas paintings in" That was where the page ended, right in the middle of the sentence. Maybe page two said something about Sarah. Maybe not. My father hadn't said anything about going to Paris in his letters to me.

Maybe it didn't make any difference what my father said about me or didn't say. After all, if somebody invited *me* to go to Paris and I decided to go, I would run to the door every time it opened and tell whoever came in, *I'm going to Paris!* My mother hadn't even stood up from her easel when I got home, and all she had said was, "Cookies on the counter, Sarah. Wash your hands before you eat."

Usually, for us to have cookies is exciting, but not even chocolate cake with ice cream would have interested me right then. When my mother called upstairs, "Sarah? Don't you want a snack before you do your homework?" I told her I wasn't hungry.

"I have a test tomorrow," I said.

"Come down and at least drink a glass of milk," she told me. "Brains need food."

Maybe, I thought, my mother wants me to come down so she can tell me we're going to France! If I don't breathe till I get to the kitchen, she will be waiting to tell me that! When I got to the kitchen, the page was gone. My mother had filled a glass with milk and left it for me on the counter. I emptied it down the sink and went back upstairs.

At supper she didn't say much and I didn't, either, because all I could think of was, Are you going? and, of course, I couldn't ask her. Reading my parents' mail is totally not allowed. Now I can see why.

14

The Next Book

Pat Hardy had a date! Annette told me the first thing when I got to her house. For a minute I even forgot wondering whether my father misses me, what page two of his letter about Paris said, whether my mother has answered, and what. I had asked my mother would we be home for Christmas several times before I read page one of my father's letter, so I wouldn't be giving away what I knew about Paris if I asked her again, I had decided. Her answer, though, was not a whole lot better than *We'll see* (or *You will find out before you're married*). "I am considering two or three possibilities for Christmas," she said. "I'll tell you what I decide the day I know myself." At least Annette's news put that out of my mind for a while.

"I won't get a lesson this afternoon," Annette said, "but we'll muck as usual. Pat's going to leave our money with Cousin Augusta."

"Will she wear a dress?" I asked.

"Cousin Augusta?"

Annette's Cousin Augusta is Pat's mother. "No, *Pat*."

"Of course. Why not?"

I couldn't imagine Pat in a dress. "Will Mrs. Hardy take us home?"

"No, my father's coming to get us."

I like Annette's father; I like her whole family. I love to imagine being home again and telling my friends about going to her house. "Mrs. Frazier was always throwing pots," I will say.

The first time Annette told me, "My mother threw two new pots yesterday," I totally didn't know what to say. I don't know what I'd do if my mother started smashing things, I thought. When my mother gets mad with me, she inspects my room. I always thought *that* was bad, I told Annette. My friends won't know any better than I did that "throwing pots" is what clay potters say for "making pots," and their eyes will get big as owls' until I've explained.

Annette says you have to have very strong hands and shoulders to throw pots. She thinks maybe that's why she takes to riding: "I've probably inherited my mother's strong hands and shoulders."

Mr. Frazier's job is insuring horses. "That takes a strong stomach," he says, "but the only other place I need strong muscles is in my cheeks." He is always smiling and telling jokes.

Mr. Frazier's hobbies are watching University of Kentucky basketball games and taking snapshots of Annette and Simms and Lulu. The University of Kentucky basketball team is the Wildcats. On his desk Mr. Frazier has pictures of his family, and a wildcat Mrs. Frazier made him out of a leftover piece of clay too small for a vase or a casserole. "She can model any animal but an invisible dragon," Annette says.

I was glad Mr. Frazier was coming for Annette and me because I think it cheers my father up when I write him Mr. Frazier's jokes.

Because Annette started mucking the same time I did, we got the stalls cleaned earlier than usual. Annette looked at her watch. "My father won't be here for half an hour," she said. "What do you want to do? If we go for our money now, we'll have to sit and talk to Cousin Augusta until he comes. I don't really mind that, but she will give us yogurt and watch us eat it, and I hate yogurt."

"Why don't you give me a riding lesson," I said. I almost choked saying it, and Annette almost choked hearing it.

"Okay," she said. "Why not?"

"I just want to learn to sit on her!" I didn't have any trouble saying *that*. "She doesn't need to gallop or canter or trot or anything, and I'm *not* going to jump any cavalletti."

"Nobody does, the first day," Annette said. She showed me how to saddle Chilly. Chilly acted the way I used to act posing for my mother: shifting her feet just when I wanted her to stand still, rolling her eyes, making a lot of disgusted breathing noises. She was quiet when we led her out to the paddock, though. I didn't put my knee in Annette's hands; I climbed up on the plank fence and got on the saddle from there. I was totally terrified. This is not worthwhile, I kept thinking. My hands were sweating and my heart was racing and my jaws were jammed together. Moving just my lips I said, "Walk her around."

It wasn't so bad. At first things looked blurry, and I couldn't dare let go of the reins long enough to wipe my eyes, but after I finally blinked them clear, I asked Annette, "Would she run, if you let her go?"

"Not unless you grip her with your knees."

I felt cold air whoosh up my legs as I jerked my knees away from Chilly's warm body. My teeth were locked again. "Let go of her, then," I managed to say.

It wasn't so bad. It wasn't so bad. Chilly walked around the paddock as if she knew what she was supposed to do. Annette said I did fine for a first time.

"I didn't do it to please Pat!" I told her. "I don't even want you to tell her. Promise."

"Okay," Annette said. "I promise I will not tell Pat."

As we led Chilly out of the paddock, Mr. Frazier was waiting for us beside his car. He drove us over to the house for our pay, and Annette didn't have to eat yogurt.

When I got home my mother was just sorting the mail. "You have four letters, Sarah," she said. "All from yourself, I'm afraid." Mrs. DeMeter is right: I-am-Rachel should take typing in school.

"They're not really from myself," I said. "Just the envelopes." I started to take them upstairs.

"Don't tell me," she said, smiling. "I can guess. You finally figured out that the way to get your friends to write you was to send them envelopes." I had never thought of that.

I know my mother. She says my mail is part of my self-space and she will never open it, but she will smile and guess until I tell her what it says. I turned around and opened one envelope. It had one of those long, printed letters in it that doesn't say anything but no. The second envelope had one of those printed *No* notes, too, and so did the third. The fourth one had my letter still in it. Somebody had written across the bottom, "Sorry, but thanks. Cute girl. You? Roger Feindish, Editor." The three pictures I had made were in there, too. I handed the whole thing to my mother. I made a face so she wouldn't think *I* thought I was cute.

My mother read my letter and Mr. Feindish's remarks. "Oh,

Sarah," she exclaimed, "you are a treasure! What ever gave you this beautiful idea?"

"I miss Dad."

"I do, too," she said.

Well, are you going to Paris? I wanted to shout, but I couldn't. "Are you going skiing with Dr. Bedford when it snows?" I asked.

"No," she said. "You don't have to worry about Dr. Bedford. He's a nice man, but he's not as clever as your father. And that's a known fact," she added, looking right at me and laughing, so I knew she meant it.

SO WAS SHE GOING TO PARIS? "So are we going," I asked, "home soon?" I held my breath.

"Oh, Sarah, hasn't Kentucky been at *all* positive for you?" my mother asked. "Haven't you related to Meterboro at all?"

"Everybody in Meterboro is related except me," I said.

My mother laughed. "Well, I'm sorry you haven't had fun, but I think it's been a learning experience, at least. I think you've grown."

"I'm half an inch taller," I said. "Maybe Dad won't know me if I grow any more before he sees me."

My mother laughed again. "I hope to have you back to your father before you're unrecognizable."

Something cold traveled up my spine. What did she mean, *have me back to my father?* Were they planning to take turns with me the way Demeter did with her daughter? My throat started to close up. "Aren't you coming with me?" I asked.

"Of course," said my mother. "But don't ask me when, because I don't know exactly. I hope I'm almost done here. As soon as my editor tells me what she thinks of this last batch I'm about to send her. . . . It would be a pity for us to get home and then find out she wants one more picture that I should have done here."

"Get home," she'd said. I swallowed a couple of times. This summer I heard her telling Dr. Bedford, "Home is where I set up my easel." After that I paid attention, and times when I would have said "back home," she would say "in New York." *Get home* was progress.

"The minute I know exactly when we're going, I'll tell you," she said. "Till then I don't want you getting all excited and thinking your Meterboro school doesn't matter. I want you to go in there and do your best every day, just as if you'll be there all year."

Grown-ups are always telling you the most exciting thing you can think of and then telling you not to get excited. We were going to go home, *both* of us. It was more exciting than Paris. I started to grin like crazy and dance around.

"Are you really desperate to leave Meterboro?" my mother asked. "Haven't you formed any relationships here you'll miss? What about Annette?"

I stopped dancing. "I will miss Annette," I said. "I'll miss her a lot. But maybe she'll come to New York sometimes. People come from everywhere to visit New York a lot more than they come from New York to visit Meterboro. And that's a known fact," I added, because I wanted my mother to laugh with me the way I had laughed with her, but she didn't seem to have heard me. She was looking at my copies of her pictures, of me on the lion, of me at the zoo, of me with my Chinatown hat.

"Now that you've learned how to pose," my mother said slowly (I didn't know she'd noticed), "what would you think of helping me write my own book? A sort of guide for children visiting New York? I could draw you at places you and I like, and you could tell me what you like about them. Then you could send a copy to all your Meterboro friends to encourage their parents to bring them to New York."

I threw my arms around her. "What a *dazz* idea!" I cried. "That would be really worthwhile! Will it be your next book?" I was almost dancing again.

"It could be our next but one."

It took me a second to notice she had said "our." I was already asking, "What's the next one?"

"What an American girl likes to do in Paris at Christmas," said my mother. "Would you like that?"

Totally yes!

15
Unexpected Development

On Monday, Mrs. DeMeter shouldn't have paid me at all, I had so much to tell her. Paris first. Then getting on Chilly. "Did you enjoy it?" she asked.

"No. But maybe it will seem like fun when I remember it in New York."

She smiled. "Lots of fun is like that."

I'm going to miss Mrs. DeMeter.

"Don't be sad," she told me. "Leaving a place is the only way to keep it from changing. If you stay you'll discover that even in one year's time, some things you liked will vanish and some things will come that you'd rather not see."

Tuesday morning when Annette stopped for me to walk to school with her, I told her what Mrs. DeMeter said. "You can find out whether she's right," Annette told me, "when you come back to visit me next summer. Can't she?" she asked my mother.

"We'll see," my mother said. I sighed, but I have learned that sometimes *We'll see* can mean yes.

"Pat said to give you this," Annette told me. She handed me an envelope marked "City-girl." Inside was a snapshot of me sitting on Chilly. "I had nothing to do with it!" said Annette. "My father took that picture while he was waiting for us day before yesterday. He developed the roll after I went to bed, and he gave your picture to Pat before I even saw it." Then her grin broke through. "I have a copy, too, though. Hope you don't mind."

Wait till she sees the picture my mother made of *her* on Chilly! If we get to go home before her birthday, I will give it to her first. I want to see her face when she sees it.

If I still hated Pat, I would send her another picture of me, a picture of me getting on a jet plane, but actually I guess I like her pretty well. If I do get to visit Annette next summer, I won't go off while Pat is giving her and Chilly their lesson.

I'm copying addresses, for mailing my Christmas presents: Annette's, of course, and Mrs. DeMeter's. I don't have to write down Mrs. Hume's. I will never forget Henry Clay Street and the Meterboro Public Library.

I can't believe I'll really be doing my Christmas shopping in France! But when I start to believe it, I know what this American girl wants to do in Paris: go to a real French pastry shop with money that I earned myself and buy real French chocolate éclairs for my father, and for my mother.

I have also copied the address of the Reverend James S. Caywood out of the Meterboro telephone directory. When my mother's next-but-one book is published, the one about kids visiting New York City, I'm going to send a copy to Australia Caywood. Inside I will write *To Frog-boy, from Sarah the Dragon Lady*.

WORLDS OF WONDER
FROM
AVON CAMELOT

THE INDIAN IN THE CUPBOARD
60012-9/$2.95US/$3.95Can
THE RETURN OF THE INDIAN
70284-3/$2.95US only

Lynne Reid Banks

"Banks conjures up a story that is both thoughtful and captivating and interweaves the fantasy with care and believability" *Booklist*

THE HUNKY-DORY DAIRY
Anne Lindbergh   70320-3/$2.50US/$3.50Can

"A beguiling fantasy...full of warmth, wit and charm"
Kirkus Reviews

THE MAGIC OF THE GLITS
C.S. Adler   70403-X/$2.50US/$3.50Can

"A truly magical book" *The Reading Teacher*

GOOD-BYE PINK PIG
C.S. Adler   70175-8/$2.50US/$2.95Can

Every fifth grader needs a friend she can count on!

Buy these books at your local bookstore or use this coupon for ordering:
....

Avon Books, Dept BP, Box 767, Rte 2, Dresden, TN 38225
Please send me the book(s) I have checked above. I am enclosing $_____
(please add $1.00 to cover postage and handling for each book ordered to a maximum of three dollars). *Send check or money order*—no cash or C.O.D.'s please. Prices and numbers are subject to change without notice. Please allow six to eight weeks for delivery.

Name _____

Address _____

City _____ State/Zip _____

Wonder 9/87

Please allow 6-8 weeks for delivery